PILATE'S CROSS

Book One in the *John Pilate Mystery Series*

J. ALEXANDER GREENWOOD

PILATE'S CROSS

Book One in the *John Pilate Mystery Series*

J. ALEXANDER GREENWOOD

Original Copyright © 2010 by J. Alexander Greenwood

Revised third edition Copyright © 2019 Caroline Street Press

All rights reserved.

ISBN: 978-1-79-681649-5

Cover designed by Jason McIntyre
TheFarthestReaches.com

Books by J. Alexander Greenwood

Pilate's Cross
Pilate's Cross: The Audiobook
Pilate's Key
Pilate's Ghost
Pilate's Blood
Pilate's 7
Pilate's Rose

Big Cabin & Dispatches from the West
(with Robert E. Trevathan)

Non-Fiction
Kickstarter Success Secrets
Kickstarter Success Secrets: The Audiobook

Visit www.PilatesCross.com
for the latest updates, merchandise and the Clues Blog.

Dedicated to my wife Stephanie, our daughter Caroline, and my late grandfather, author Robert E. Trevathan.

CONTENTS

ACKNOWLEDGMENTS

Thanks to my draft readers, Kristin, Scott, Terry, Mary, and Stephanie. Without your invaluable critiques, there would be no *Pilate's Cross*.

Thanks to Jason McIntyre for a stunning new cover and book design! Special thanks to my extended family for their love, continual support, and encouragement in all my endeavors.

Thanks to my editor, Autumn C., who helped make this book better with her revisions.

To those who have been quick with a kind word, an offer to help, or for simply telling me "Yes, it can be done…and you can do it!" many, many thanks! You know who you are, and you are much appreciated.

PROLOGUE

November 26, 1963

Dr. Brady Bernard tied his bowtie as he gazed in the mirror of his small deco tiled bathroom. A breeze blew in over his shoulder from the window above the bathtub—a window he'd always kept open "just a crack" after a faulty gas heater in the bathroom nearly asphyxiated him and his wife a few months prior. Unlike the shattered nuptial union that had also nearly succeeded in suffocating him over time, the good doctor had at least managed to repair the heater.

He slipped the burgundy tie ends together just as he had thousands of times before. A jaunty bow formed around his neck, and his sagging skin fell around it. Bernard adjusted the wire- framed glasses on his ruddy face, slipped his suspenders over his shoulders, and ran a comb through his thinning, pomaded hair.

He glanced quickly at the headlines of the two-day-old newspaper crumpled on the floor beside the toilet:

KENNEDY SLAIN ON DALLAS STREET.

Bernard heaved a disgusted sigh. Like so many others, he liked President Kennedy. The assassination had a surprisingly strong effect on him, though not for the typical reasons anyone might suspect. The stairs creaked and groaned under his 260-pound frame. From the landing, through his leaded-glass window on his front door, he saw gentle snowflakes falling. Bernard slipped into his jacket, followed by his overcoat. He dimmed the lamp on the end table, opened the front door, and stepped one foot outside, but then stopped abruptly. "Oh yes!" he said. He turned quickly on the ball of his foot and marched across the living room to a seven-drawer oak desk. For the first time in months, he took notice of the framed motto he'd hung over his desk several years ago:

An Indian scalps his enemy...a white man skins his friend.

Dr. Bernard sighed at the bitter truth, removed a key from his pocket, and used it to open the center drawer, pulling it about an inch out of its resting place. Grunting as he folded his heavy body over, he reached to the bottom left-hand drawer and opened it. From that drawer, he scooped up something heavy, then stood upright and closed it gently with his cap-toed shoe. He locked the center drawer again and walked into the snowy campus world at his teachers' college near the banks of the Missouri River.

Dottie Mostek sat, ramrod straight, at her desk, her eyes rimmed with red from shedding so many tears on behalf of the deceased President Kennedy, whose funeral had taken place just the day before. Her dark hair, which she'd styled in proper Jackie form for the past three years, was as disheveled as her emotional state, a careless mess. She just could not force herself to care about styling her hair; in the grand scheme of things, it seemed so trivial.

She touched her hand to her chin and glanced at a newspaper that offered grainy grayscale photos taken at the funeral. *Bobby looked so devastated, and John-John's salute was heartbreaking.*

Out of respect for the fallen Commander in Chief, classes had been canceled, and the school had been closed to students for the week, but today administrative staff were expected back to work. Dottie was relieved there would be no students. *I can sure use the peace and quiet,* she thought with a defeated sigh, glancing in her compact mirror at the destroyed mop on her head.

Earlier, Dr. Walker Keillor had quietly slipped in. At the sight of her stricken expression, he consoled, "It's a sad day for us all, Dottie. Try to get a hold of yourself."

She nodded at the other chief executive in her life, the president of Cross College, and sat up straighter in her chair. Next, she dutifully attempted to type a memo as President Keillor disappeared behind his office door. She admired Dr. Keillor, a reserved and thoughtful man who had been in education most of his sixty-two years.

Downstairs, Dean Gareth Kennedy had been spending the last few moments reminiscing with his secretary, Grace Hamilton, about the time he'd met JFK himself on a train right after the war. He regaled her with the tale of borrowing a newspaper from the rail-thin, nearly-crippled Navy hero. "He said 'showr' in that Boston accent of his and handed it to me," Kennedy said. "I introduced myself, and that was when he told me he was Jack Kennedy. That's why I remember meeting him. We had a laugh about being related or something like that." He paused a moment, tapping his finger on the Kansas City newspaper that lay open on his desk, plastered with photos of the slain president's memorial service. "I, uh…" His voice trailed off.

Grace looked at the steno pad in her hands.

Kennedy shook his head, wiped his glasses, and told Grace to tell the two typewriter salesmen in his outer office that he would be with them in a few minutes.

She closed his door quietly and returned to her desk.

Walter Mackey, of the Westside Typewriter and Office Company, waited patiently in Dr. Kennedy's outer office, seated in a worn wooden chair. Next to him sat Thomas Guthrie, his new trainee. Mackey was entering his twentieth year in the sales game, and this week he was tasked with showing the freshly-discharged-from-the- Army kid, Guthrie, the ropes. On the way over from the city, he'd filled Guthrie in on the sad story of Cross Township, telling the wide-eye rookie how Cross had once rested close to the banks of the Missouri River—until the Great Flood of 1943 rerouted the mighty Missouri and quashed Cross's ambitions of economic glory. Now it was a small, anemic college town a mile from the river and two miles off the beaten track of State Highway 9. "But they've still got a college there, and colleges need office equipment, one way or another," he'd explained to Guthrie.

"Dr. Kennedy will see you in a few minutes, gentlemen."

"Thank you, ma'am," Mackey said.

Guthrie smiled back at her as well. *A little too big*, Mackey thought.

"If you're in a hurry, you might want to go upstairs to the commerce office to handle the past billing," Grace said. "Then you could come back about the new typewriter order."

"Aw, that's okay. We can wait," Mackey said.

Guthrie nodded assent, sliding his beaten-up leather satchel on the floor beside his chair.

Grace sat down. "He has an appointment with one of our professors at 8:15, but it shouldn't take long," she said.

The men nodded; they knew the drill.

A few awkward minutes passed after the campus bell rang 8:15 a.m.

Mackey looked at his watch, then at Grace. "Terrible what happened in Dallas," the salesman said, trying to make conversation.

Guthrie nodded in silent agreement, his face grim.

"Yes," Grace said. She was the picture of efficiency, and any grief she had for President Kennedy—or nearly any emotion at all—was reserved for her husband and dog to see.

Mackey was not one to be ignored, however, which served him well in the sales business. "Just awful. I'm glad they got that bastard Oswald," Mackey said.

Grace jumped a bit at "bastard."

"Oh sorry, ma'am. Pardon my French, but this whole thing's just so upsettin'."

Grace stood and offered a simple, "Yes." She looked back at her boss's door. "Perhaps Dr. Kennedy can see you since Dr. Bernard seems to be running late today," she offered, wanting to get them out of her lobby so they'd stop distracting her from her work. She knocked quietly at his door and slipped in.

Mackey and Guthrie stood up and took a step toward Kennedy's door.

The double-doors rattled as a tall, portly man in a snow-speckled overcoat barreled into the outer office. He eyed the two men for a second and said, "I'm first. I have an appointment."

Grace returned from Kennedy's office. "Oh, Dr. Bernard," she said, not looking him in the eye. "Dr. Kennedy is ready to see you and has been expecting you. Please go on in."

Bernard nodded and walked past Grace and the salesmen. He quietly closed Dr. Kennedy's door behind him.

Mackey whistled. "Boy, that's a friendly fella, huh?" he said.

Grace looked at her desktop as if to make it clear she wasn't there to make excuses or explanations for anyone. "Dr. Bernard has been...well..." She cleared her throat and leaned forward toward the men.

In turn, the salesmen leaned forward in the creaky old chairs, eager to hear some rare gossip from the usually Sphinx-like Grace.

She had just opened her ruby-red lips to speak when the air in the room crackled with an explosive series of five sounds.

Mackey froze.

Grace jumped.

Guthrie launched from his chair. "Was that...gunshots?" he said.

Dr. Kennedy's office door opened, and Bernard calmly strode into the outer office, closing the door behind him with his left hand, holding a distinctive German Luger pistol that was partially obscured under his coat with the right. A sickening sulfurous smell followed him.

Guthrie started toward the professor, but Bernard raised the gun at the veteran. In the next instant, his left hand instinctively jolted toward his eyeglasses, which had faint red specks on the lenses.

Everyone froze for a bizarre two seconds of silence before Bernard walked past them into the hallway.

Grace rushed to Kennedy's door and saw him splayed like a marionette with clipped strings on the floor beside his desk. His head rested at an odd angle of contortion against a radiator on the wall. He had a small, almost bloodless hole above his right eye. In contrast, a jagged crevasse where his nose was supposed to be bled like an open floodgate down his face, crimson staining the white, starched collar of his shirt. His right hand was also bloody and mangled; the bullet had obviously torn through it when he tried to cover his face in self-defense. Droplets of blood covered the photo of President Kennedy on the newspaper lying across his desk.

"He's been shot!" Grace choked out, stating the obvious.

Mackey burst into the room, saw Kennedy, and threw up on his own shoes.

"I knew they was gunshots," Guthrie said, whistling and patting his pockets for a pack of cigarettes.

Dottie heard what sounded like a series of thumping sounds from downstairs, but she thought little of it. She continued typing her memo until Dr. Bernard, who had calmly slipped into the room and up to her desk, interrupted her. She noted that he was wearing his overcoat and was wiping his eyeglass lenses with a monogrammed handkerchief. "Oh, Dr. Bernard, you startled me."

Bernard didn't look at her; he simply continued to clean his glasses. "He in?"

"Um, yes he is. You can go on in if you'd like," she said, keenly aware of Keillor's open-door policy with faculty, even faculty whose contracts had been terminated effective the end of semester.

Bernard grunted, put his glasses back on, and stepped toward Keillor's office. Then, he suddenly stopped. Without turning around, he spoke in monotone, "They shoot presidents these days." Then he jammed his right hand into his pocket and went in.

Dottie shivered at the emotionless announcement and looked back to her typewriter. She glanced up a second later and noticed that Bernard had not closed the door as he normally would. She craned her neck to peer into President Keillor's office. In a split second, she convinced herself that her overwrought emotions stemming from the JFK assassination had rendered her eyes unreliable. *Surely Dr. Bernard is not pointing a pistol at the head of Cross College President Walker Keillor. I must be... seeing things.*

The chain reaction of cartridge ignition rocketed the bullet from the barrel into Keillor's right eye socket.

Dottie screamed hysterically at the grim reality as Bernard took his leave, walking silently past her desk and out the door.

Bernard trudged across the snowy oval in front of the Administration building. The Luger was warm and felt nice in his pocket, a reprieve against the chilly air. The campus seemed airless and deserted to him. The carillon bells played a Christmas carol just as he reached his own front door. He shed his overcoat, draped it over the banister, then carefully removed the Luger from his pocket and walked to the desk.

He unlocked the center drawer just as he had earlier, then opened the bottom left-hand drawer, from which he retrieved a box of cartridges. He dropped the spent shells from the Luger's magazine into a wicker wastebasket beside the desk. He paused for a moment, looking at the weapon he'd personally taken from the stiff, dead hands of a German officer in a crumbling Berlin tenement. That officer's face had been left with a hole in it, too, not unlike Dean Kennedy's.

He methodically loaded the pistol, then set it on the desk and removed a piece of paper from the center drawer. It was his last letter, already typed:

> *Mr. Benton,*
>
> *Please take charge. Use Nathaniel's Funeral Home of Goss City. Services should run about $600. Cremate and scatter ashes from the bridge over the Missouri, at night, under the cover of darkness.*
>
> *Let only one person know what you have done.*
>
> *I require no funeral services or other fanciful memorials. No relatives need be notified of my demise other than my wife, wherever that harpy now resides.*
>
> *Stay in my house at night or get someone until things quiet down. Somebody might try to cause trouble.*
>
> *You will be paid for your faithful service in these matters.*
>
> *Take care of my office and bring everything down to the house.*

He signed it with his fountain pen, blotted it, and placed it before him on the desk. He reread it carefully, then wrote a postscript under his signature:

P.S. *Wally tried to fire the wrong person.*

Bernard rose from the chair, walked across the drab hooked rug, and placed the letter in its center. He capped his fountain pen and placed it on top of the letter. He removed his eyeglasses and put them in the breast pocket of his jacket breast pocket. As absently as he had tied his bowtie that morning, he placed the warm, acrid barrel of the German gun in his mouth and squeezed the trigger without a second thought.

November 29, 1963

Grif Nathaniel tapped the ashes from his cigarette into the open cardboard cylinder on the desk in front of him. The cigarette ash was finer and darker than the mortal remains of Dr. Brady Bernard, which had the appearance of fireplace ash mixed with chips of rock. The chips were not rocks at all, of course, but the remnants of the departed Bernard's bones. "All men are cremated equal," he said aloud, smiling and remembering the joy the distasteful but clever pun had brought to his father, Martin.

He leaned back in his chair, swinging his feet on the desk of the funeral home, with a pre-assassination issue of *Life* magazine resting on his knees. He had known the late Dr. Bernard from his psychology class. He remembered the man as a boring lecturer who would intentionally drop pencils so he could sneak peeks up the front row of coed skirts. Grif always thought it was funny that the strangest prof on campus taught psych. The old bird's wife had left him a few months prior, and word around campus was that Bernard's boss, Dean Kennedy, had the okay from President Keillor to fire him.

Grif leaned forward, exhaling smoke and stubbing the cigarette out in a small pan spirited from the embalming table. *Life* flopped to the morgue floor as he reached for the town's twice- weekly newspaper, the *Cross Courier*. He scanned the paper. Accounts of the Cross College president's murder had even bumped the United States President's murder off the front page— at least locally. President Keillor and Dean Kennedy were dead on the scene, and Bernard had been found dead in his living room, killed by his own hand with the same Kraut gun. He'd left a peculiar suicide note, along with the fountain pen he used to sign his name that last time.

The newspaper did not reveal the contents of the note, but Grif knew. Sheriff Scovill had told Martin Nathaniel that the letter left strict instructions for cremation and how to dispose of Bernard's effects. Scovill also intimated that there was a bizarre postscript, but he would say nothing further about it.

Grif had asked his high school buddy, Morgan Scovill, a member of the "social club" known as the Cross Cavaliers, what he knew, but Morgan was as stubborn and tight-lipped as his father, the sheriff. "Come on, Morg! We're Cavaliers. We have no secrets between us, right?" Grif had coaxed, trying to revive the camaraderie of the gang from high school.

Morgan Scovill had simply shaken his head and said, "Oh, but we do have secrets, Grif…and be glad we do."

"Crazy sum'bitch," was all Sheriff Scovill had allowed Grif beyond the press accounts. After his firsthand observation of Bernard's handiwork on the heads of Keillor and Kennedy, Grif had to agree. Even with Martin's artistry with mortician's wax and makeup, closed caskets were the order of the day for both funerals. In his twenty-two years growing up in the family business, Griffin Nathaniel had seen his share of dead bodies—none worse than those mangled by combines or car wrecks. However, in his opinion, there was something far more gruesome about a bullet hole in the face and a blown-out skull.

"Griffin?" Martin Nathaniel called to his son from the stairs. "Son, you down there?"

"Yes, Dad," Grif said, waving at the smoke in the air.

Martin descended the stairs, looking paler than usual. Admittedly, the man could have walked right out of Central Casting to play the part of a mortuary director even on his best day, but on this day, he looked flushed, perhaps even ill. His thin fingers nervously smoothed his black frock. "Where's Dr. Bernard?" he said in the way they always referred to the deceased, regardless of whether they were on an exam table or in a jar.

"Right here," Grif said, glancing down at the open cylinder before him.

"Oh good."

"Dad, you okay?" Grif said, unused to seeing his father's studied reserve shaken and bothered by the man's profuse and uncharacteristic perspiration.

"Yeah. Just came down the stairs a little too fast, I suppose," he said, his face morphing into the mask of disengaged kindness that he usually saved for the customers. "Do me a favor, son. Uh, I need you to go to the bank and deposit this check from the Harrisons. I have a feeling we shouldn't hold on to it for too long."

Grif thought it an unusual request, as the Harrisons had been a local farm family in the area since the days before Moses, and they'd always paid their bills. "Uh, sure, Dad," Grif said, pulling his jacket on and carefully nudging the *Life* magazine under the desk with his foot. He took the check from his father's bony hand.

"Thank ya, son. I'll uh...well, I'm gonna seal up Dr. Bernard." "His wife gonna claim him anytime soon?" Grif asked, halfway up the stairs.

"No," Martin said without turning away from the open cylinder. "Nope, I don't think so. We'll hang on to him a while in case she changes her mind. Now please be on your way."

Grif hurried up the stairs to find his overcoat for the chilly trip to the bank.

Martin's hand shakily fished into his frock coat. From a buttoned interior pocket, he retrieved a small brown ledger, held together with a fat rubber band. He fingered the rubber band a moment and looked at the crematory oven on the other side of the room. It had been fired up early yesterday for Dr. Bernard and was still quite warm. Martin took a step toward the crematory until he was stopped by Grif's shout from upstairs.

"Dad! The mayor's here and wants to see you. He says it's urgent."

Martin started, and the shaking in his hands worsened. The ledger suddenly seemed as hot as a coal from the oven. He hurriedly dropped it in the cylinder of Brady Bernard's ashes, sending a plume of dusty remains into the air. He then sealed the package with packing tape. "I'll be right up," his voice quavered.

The cylinder of ashes was still warm to the touch as he carried them to a small closet in the basement. He felt in the dark for the light chain and pulled it. Martin slid Dr. Brady Bernard's ashes onto the shelf next to rolls of toilet paper and some dusty plastic flowers. He pulled the chain again to turn out the naked light bulb and closed the door. As he climbed the stairs to the parlor, the unmistakable voice of Mayor Ollie Olafson greeted him.

"Marty, we need to talk."

CHAPTER ONE

THE NEW MILLENNIUM

John Pilate's face loomed in the bathroom mirror, illuminated by a single sickening scented candle flickering on the toilet tank.

The three a.m. antidepressant withdrawal-induced orbit around the apartment had ravaged his features.

He stared in the mirror at his own dark eyes. The sleepless house, converted to apartments, creaked under his feet as Pilate shifted his weight from side to side, testing his profile in the glass. His brushed aside a lock of brown hair that hung over one eye. *Man, I need a haircut. And a shave. And a damn job.*

Drips from the tap caressed the porcelain, wearing it down at a millennial pace. He twisted the tap hard to stop it.

"Goddamn," he said, blowing out the candle. His eyes adjusted as he stumbled down the hallway to go back to bed. His side of the iron-framed full-size was rumpled; hers was almost smooth. The empty bed bathed in the moonlight only served to remind Pilate of his wife's absence. He couldn't help but recall the sight of her bare, taut body in the moonlit lake the first time they'd made love. Memories of her came and went often; this was one of the "went" periods, when Pilate tried fooling himself into believing she was coming back. "Samantha," he said aloud, his voice chalky, startling even his own ears.

He carefully slid back into bed, careful not to disturb her side. He pretended to sleep in hopes that the sandman would be drawn to him, if only for a few minutes, but he soon gave up on his quest for rest. Pilate leaned his head on his hand, his eyes drowsing, the sun almost up. His temples throbbed, and his waking dreams started at the beginning like a skipping record.

He had begged her. "Please! We can fix this…I can live with…" He didn't know what he was saying. He saw something in her eyes he could not comprehend.

She touched his cheek with her thin, mocha-colored fingers and mouthed, *"Goodbye, John."*

He closed his eyes as if the sunlight was an insult.

Pilate brewed coffee. Books were piled on the floor; an ashtray full of sunflower seed shells lay partially dumped out on the carpet; and a stack of compact disks littered the floor in front of the entertainment center. Dishes in the sink were rinsed but not really clean. The refrigerator chilled food that held no enticement. He replayed the answering machine message he'd received yesterday, only to once again hear the joyless, robotic voice of a joyless, robotic bill collector who insisted on mispronouncing his last name.

It's Pilate, asshole—like the Roman governor, not the damned workout. Ever read the Bible? Pilate thought as he thumbed through his mail, which mostly consisted of Sam's credit card bills that she had foisted upon him. He stacked them on the dining room table, assuming they'd make a lovely bonfire on Guy Fawkes Day. Colin Hay's "No Sign of Yesterday" blared from the stereo.

He went to the bathroom, stripped, and stood under the showerhead. Hot, steamy water drilled into his sandy brown head, rolling down his soft but flat belly, over his waist, and down his thighs. Water fled to the end of his penis and drained off like rain from a broken gutter. He rubbed soap between his fingers and thought of a tropical island with brown, pleasing women, tall drinks with funny names, and his feet buried in sand up to the ankle.

The water turned tepid, then cool. As the chill overtook him, he thought of the past few weeks, the finality of Samantha's words and the cancer scare that had led to the removal of his tonsils. *These damn ten-year-olds getting excited about devouring all the Jell-O they can eat in the hospital. God, my throat still hurts.* Pilate crouched by the drain until the shower water turned intolerably cold.

He stepped out and toweled off. Steam obscured his image in the mirror. He examined his razor: bristles and excess shaving cream clotted the blades like a scab. Pilate dropped the cartridge in the trash and found a fresh one in a drawer, which was still filled with Samantha's feminine totems: makeup, tampons, Midol, and that sinister-looking contraption that she'd bravely used to curled her eyelashes.

He jerked the drawer out of the cabinet and threw it into the small trashcan in the corner of the bathroom. The drawer left a satisfying gouge in the wall it hit before landing in the basket, and pills and eyeliner scattered about.

"Damn it!" he shouted. His throat instantly felt as if he had gargled glass. Three weeks after the surgery, Pilate's throat still burned. Along with his tonsils, he had shed eighteen pounds.

He was also dead broke and very nearly out on his ass. Pilate had sheepishly borrowed a little from his fixed-income parents to pay the bills while he was in hospital, but that money was perilously close to gone; soon, he would have to vacate the apartment he had shared with Samantha. Where he would go remained undecided. However, for another five days, he had the place to himself.

Pilate noticed the blink of his answering machine light; someone had called while he was in the shower and left a message. He pushed the play button, bracing himself for the bored authority in the voice of yet another disgruntled bill collector.

"Mr. Pilate, this is Dr. Peter Trevathan at Cross College," a voice fairly crusty with cantankerousness purred. "We'd like you to come up…to work with us. We feel you will be an excellent addition to our faculty."

The offer was to start as an instructor in speech and creative writing at the small Midwestern land-grant college. Pilate had applied online in the spur of the moment when he'd seen the wanted ad in a public library copy of the *Chronicle of Higher Education*. After all, he had to submit a few applications a week to keep his unemployment checks coming, pitiful as they were. On a lark, he'd applied to the college, which was 500 miles away, with no real anticipation of an interview, much less an offer.

The previous week, he'd croaked through two phone interviews, shared a portfolio of old clips, and apparently caught the college in the middle of a dearth of instructors. Reading between the lines of what Trevathan had told him, it seemed a fairly new president at the college had fired, pissed off, or simply alienated enough faculty members that they needed warm bodies to fill the slots for the spring semester.

Pilate told Trevathan he could be there just after Christmas.

He didn't mention his recent surgery.

"Do you have a cold?" Trevathan asked.

"No. It's just a sore throat," Pilate said.

He decided he could crash at his folks' place for a few weeks before the move, and they were happy to comply. For several days, he busied himself packing boxes for the move north. *North to the new job. North away from Samantha…Away.*

CHAPTER TWO

Cross College sent a small check to help him with moving expenses, but by the time Pilate paid for a U-Haul van, a trailer for his car, and all the other relocation hoopla he had to take care of, he had a meager $145 left; worse, it was going to be a long time until his first payday in February.

His mother hugged him tight; his father tried to put a carefully folded $100 bill in his pocket. Pilate thanked his father and slipped the money in his mother's jacket pocket without either noticing. They'd been on a fixed income for a year, ever since a factory floor accident had taken his dad out of the workforce. A small settlement and his father's shrewd investment of his pension funds had kept them from eating cat food, but Pilate wasn't going to ask for any more help. He wanted—needed—to make it under his own steam, if only to prove to himself that he could. If he ended up having to eat cat food, at least it would be cat food that he paid for himself.

"Johnny, have you been taking your pills?" His mother's face was all trepidation and concern for her second son, as mother's faces tend to be. "You know you need to stay on them."

Pilate kissed her cheek. "Yes, Mom, I have," he lied. He had not been able to afford his antidepressants for several weeks, and with no insurance and income, he had little hope of refilling his prescriptions. He silently promised his mother he would start back on them when his new insurance kicked in.

His father grasped his hand. Pilate looked into his eyes and knew his dad fervently needed him to succeed, to forget Sam and get on with his life.

"Forget her, son," he said, even though Pilate had already gotten the message before he'd even uttered the words. "You deserve to get on with your life and be happy."

Pilate nodded, playfully punched his dad's arm, and climbed into the van.

The drive took him north through miles of farmland, a flat, uneventful landscape that forced his thoughts and memories to the forefront. Whole miles passed with Pilate entranced in his reverie.

Rumble bars warned him when he migrated near the road's edge. He would smoothly pull the steering wheel of the rented truck and trailer to the left to get back in the center of the lane. He glanced over into the passenger seat of the U-Haul, where there sat the small care package of sandwiches, cookies, and sodas that his mother had thoughtfully packed up for him—another thing mothers tend to do.

Hundreds of miles passed with only the dirge of neoconservative propaganda spewing from the pathetic AM radio. Every hour or so, Pilate would turn it off for some relief from the idiocy, but quickly, the silence would become too enticing to his thoughts, so he had no choice but to return to the amusingly rank hypocrisy and jingoism.

Hours broke down into minutes, into seconds, into eternities as Pilate swam through the wintry night. Frost bit the windshield as Pilate bit into one of his mother's deviled ham sandwiches. The pain from swallowing had faded, but he still felt self-conscious about his throat. Nightmares about black, sticky bile leaking from his mouth or the horror of an exposed voice box visited his sleep often.

He had a guilty pang as he pulled over onto what was euphemistically called a "scenic overlook," shrugged into his well-worn Hugo Boss black overcoat and stepped into the deserted parking area. He patted his pockets for a half-pack of cigarettes, snatched one with trembling fingers, and poked it into his mouth. Pilate quickly lit it, inhaled, and tried to ignore the psychosomatic panic that cancer cells were waiting for this last puff to bloom in his throat. Neurotic, quick puffs followed, smoke and warm breath visible in the frigid night air. The sound of semi trucks on the highway Dopplered in and out of hearing range. He finished half the cigarette and flicked the rest away as he swallowed gulps of the cold air as if that could somehow neutralize the toxic crap he'd just inhaled.

Pilate walked around the truck and trailer; making certain his black Grand Am GT was still secure. He climbed into the warm cab of the truck and eased it back onto the interstate.

Not too long later, he branched off an interstate onto a narrower state highway. Remnants from recent snowfalls lined the roads, and icy, denuded cornfields glowed eerily in the moonlight.

He crammed three cigarette-taste-killing mints into his mouth and peered into the darkness. It was nearing eleven p.m., and fatigue was setting in. By his calculations, he had at least five more hours to go before he arrived at Cross. The truth was, he felt no real urgency to get there.

A scandal of neon mounted on a billboard pointed to an Indian casino just five miles off the highway. The sign indicated that there was a hotel there, and Pilate was certain it couldn't be nearly as depressing as the bile on the radio.

Even at such a late hour on a weekday, the casino parking lot was jammed with all sizes of pickup trucks and SUVs. The majority of vehicles, however, were the kind of beat-up, throwaway cars American automakers had shat out of their factories in the seventies and eighties.

Pilate wandered in through the door that was held open by an aged man wearing an ill-fitting white security uniform shirt and a cheap badge. He was equipped with a walkie-talkie.

The din of slot machines, Muzak, and the chatter of hundreds of gamblers assaulted Pilate's ears before he ended his walk through a long hallway to the casino floor.

In the casino, his eyes absorbed the lights of the slots, the gaudy signs, the sequined vests of the waitresses, and the crooked, toothy grins of table dealers, shuffling their decks with ease.

He smelled the carcinogenic bouquet of a hundred cigarettes being smoked at once. His pulse raced. Pilate had never been much of a gambler, especially since his home state would have nothing to do with organized, legal gambling. His forays into stacks of chips, showgirls, gout-ridden retirees and massive buffets were limited to Las Vegas. But here, in the middle of nowhere, basking in the glow of neon-splashed icy fields was a place where one could easily pick his or her own pocket.

Pilate snapped out of his thoughts when he realized he was standing too close behind a table playing $10 Blackjack hands.

A grizzled man with a roadmap of creases in his tanned, leathery face glared over his shoulder.

"Sorry," Pilate said, stepping away. His thoughts leapt to his wallet. *I've got $145, but I need a warm place to sleep.* He checked with the Native American girl at the front desk, who told him they did have vacancies. That was the good news. The bad news was that those rooms started at $115 a night. "I'll think about it and might be back," he said.

And think about it he did. *There's always the road. A few more hours would put me right on the campus. Sure, I'd be early and have to wait a while to get the keys to my apartment in faculty housing, but I could wait it out in the early morning cold, or...*

Pilate wandered around the casino, slipping stray nickels into slots. A waitress with a face like a weather-beaten shingle brought him a vodka Seven. He lit a cigarette and orbited the blackjack tables while he downed the lemony-limey vodka.

He ultimately eased into a $10 blackjack table between a porcine older lady with a supernaturally red coif and an old man with wisps of white hair sprouting from his ears and collar. Both had small stacks of black, white, and green chips in front of them.

The dealer welcomed Pilate to the table as he scooped up the losing bets from the other two players.

"Hi," Pilate said, suddenly feeling very vulnerable. He laid three $20 bills on the felt near the words "Dealer Must Hit Soft 17."

"Changing $60!" the dealer said over his shoulder.

A strikingly attractive Native American woman pit boss insouciantly glanced at Pilate, then nodded to the dealer.

The dealer expertly stacked six $10 chips in front of Pilate's position. "Good luck, sir."

The old man nodded at Pilate, and the woman ignored him, instead shuffling her chips in one of her veiny hands.

Pilate placed a $10 chip as his bet, and the other players did the same. *Not too many high rollers sit at the double sawbuck tables,* Pilate realized.

All the same, he felt his pulse quicken as a king went to Big Red, a shitty deuce was thrown at him, and an ace was turned for the old man to his left.

The old man barely moved.

The woman toyed with her chips.

The dealer turned up an ace.

Pilate lit a cigarette. "Shit," he said, louder than he intended. The pit boss cast a glare his way, to which Pilate flashed an apologetic look as he took another drag on the cigarette.

"Insurance?" the dealer said in much the same way someone would say *"Excuse me"* if they burped.

No one took the sucker bet.

The dealer checked his cards and looked at the three players apologetically. He flipped a king: blackjack.

Big Red got a nine; Old Man River got a queen—a push. Pilate got a pathetic seven.

He took a choppy, cleansing breath as the dealer snatched up his chip. "Let's see if you can do better this time," Pilate said.

Big Red nodded in agreement.

The shingle-faced waitress dropped another vodka Seven beside Pilate.

He fished in his pockets and found $1 for her.

"Thanks, hon," she said.

Pilate noticed a pale, two-inch scar on one of her freckled breasts, pushed up grotesquely by her tight, sequined vest. In the next second, he chided himself for paying more attention to the sagging boob of the waitress than to his dwindling stack of chips. He glanced around quickly before slipping another $10 clay chip down for his bet.

Big Red did the same; Old Man River doubled his bet.

This time, the dealer had a six; Big Red a seven; Pilate a ten; and Old Man River an eight.

The dealer took his hole card.

Big Red hit for another six. Then she hit again, gaining a queen. "Bust," the dealer said with all the sincerity of Alex Trebek on Jeopardy.

Big Red made a sound somewhere between a snort and a cough and looked away as the dealer scooped up her bet and cards.

"Double down?"

Pilate looked up into the dealer's vacuous eyes, and when he did, his pulse quickened with the thrill of the temptation. "What the hell?" Pilate slipped his last chip beside the first.

The dealer flipped a card, a nine.

Nineteen? Not bad. Not the best, but not bad. Pilate felt like he could hear only the sound of his own heart beating, as if the slots and all the people had slidden into the Twilight Zone and were no longer actually present.

The dealer moved on to Old Man River, flopping down a queen. "Humph," the man said, waving off another card.

The dealer flipped his card over, a seven. He could not stop until he hit seventeen or above, so he took another card.

For a millisecond, Pilate could feel the win, but that victorious sensation drained out of him like piss down his leg when the next card was an eight. *Twenty-one. Damn him.*

The dealer had drawn twenty-one the hard way, and in just two hands, Pilate had blown almost his entire stake. He now lacked enough money for a hotel room, and he knew the solace of free drinks would end the second he stopped laying down the coin. Pilate hung his head a moment.

"Sorry, sir," the dealer said again, interrupting Pilate's one- man pity party, the rote false sincerity perhaps tinged with an honest apology for the bad luck. "You made a good play there. Took balls, mister."

"Thanks," Pilate said, standing up.

The dealer started to write him off with a monotone "Have a good night" when Pilate reached into his pocket and placed $75 on the table.

"That's the spirit!" Old Man River said, flashing a tombstone-toothed smile. "Like I said, you got balls."

"Changing $75!" the dealer called. The pit boss nodded at Pilate, her eyes narrowing.

Pilate pulled another drag out of the cigarette, slugged down the rest of the vodka, and slapped all $75 worth of chips on the felt.

"Sir, you sure you want to—" the dealer began.

Pilate cut him off with a determined nod.

Big Red looked irritated at the dealer. "Let him bet. He's bad luck. Maybe he'll get it over with and leave."

Pilate smiled at the old bag. "By all means."

Old Man River glared at the woman. "Mariellen, you are as big a bitch today as you were the hateful day I married you."

She glared back at him. "Oh shut up, Walter," she said, betting another $10 chip.

Walter bet the same, drawing his John Deere green hat low over his eyes.

The dealer snickered, waited for betting to cease, and then dealt himself a jack. Quickly, a seven went to Mariellen, an ace to Pilate, and a four to Walter.

"Whoa, Nellie!" said the dealer. He checked it in the table's built-in mirror.

"Insurance?"

"Shit," Pilate whispered.

"S'okay, kid," Walter said.

All waved off the sucker bet. The dealer let his cards rest: no blackjack.

Pilate sighed unintentionally loudly in an odd stuttering manner. The dealer offered Mariellen a card. She stabbed at the table with her fake pink fingernail. He obliged with a three. She was now in position for a good outcome—possibly even a blackjack if an ace turned up—no worse than a push if a face card or a ten decided to make an appearance. She stabbed the table again.

The dealer flicked a four down.

Walter guffawed into his sleeve.

"Fourteen," the dealer said. He was showing a jack, so she had no choice but to take another card.

The suicide king's visage appeared.

Big Red Mariellen cursed, grabbed her purse, and stood. "Walter, let's go."

"But I gotta finish my hand."

Only first it was Pilate's turn, and he had no patience with Mariellen and Walter anymore.

The dealer flipped down a nine.

"Ten or twenty!" the dealer called. At best, he would win, and at worst, it would be a push.

Pilate gave the cut-off sign.

Walter was given a six, then an eight, and he decided to sit on his eighteen.

The dealer flipped over a six, making a sixteen and forcing him to hit again.

Pilate's stomach dropped.

The dealer snatched another card from the six-deck shoe and slapped it onto the felt. "Four! Twenty!" He tapped his knuckles on the table in front of Pilate; it was a push. He snatched up Walter's chip.

Walter stood, flipped a George at the dealer, patted Pilate on the back with a wink, and ambled after Mariellen, who was idling on her cankles at the casino door.

"Just you and me now, sir," the dealer said.

Pilate read the name of the dealer. "Jake, I know this isn't your problem, but I've had nothing but bad luck for the past couple years," Pilate said, lighting another cigarette. He gingerly picked up the $75 in chips and held them in his right hand.

"Really? Sorry to hear that, sir. Shuffling!" He expertly piled the spent cards into an intricate series of shuffles before packing them into the shoe.

The pit boss nodded and wrote something on her tally sheet. "Yeah," Pilate said, taking a long puff, "and I got one last chance given to me recently."

"Oh yeah?" Jake said; his eye flashed with rare interest, more characteristic of bartenders than blackjack dealers.

"Yeah." Pilate tapped his ashes into the tray beside him as the waitress brought him another drink. "Ma'am, I'll be right with you with a tip. Can you come back?"

She frowned but managed a weak but sweet "Sure honey" as she walked away.

"Well, I think this here hand of blackjack might set the tone for a whole new chapter in my life."

"If you say so, sir." Jake smiled. "Are you ready to begin that chapter?"

"Yes, Jake. I am," Pilate said, stacking the $75 bet carefully in the betting circle again.

Jake sighed deeply, his left hand reaching for the shoe.

Jake's face was priceless when the blackjack bloomed in front of Pilate.

Pilate's head dropped slightly. He couldn't believe he had a caught a break; he hadn't really convinced himself that that would be the case. Pilate took his winnings, a tidy sum, and stood up. He flipped a $5 chip at Jake.

The dealer smiled. "Quite a play, sir," he said. "Quite a play indeed. Sure you want to quit now? You may be on a roll —a new chapter, like you said."

Pilate smiled.

CHAPTER THREE

The hotel room was nice in a sterile, clean, Xerox copy sort of way. Pilate poured all the shampoo into the bathtub and filled it. As usual, he failed to allow room for any cool water to mix with the hot. He eased into the steaming bath as soon as his body could stand it, his hairy legs tingling; his tail end going in not unlike Bugs Bunny into the cannibals' pot. As he acclimated, a contented sigh—again, not unlike the famous cartoon hare—escaped him.

Pilate snatched a green washcloth from the nearby basin, dipped the cloth in the water, and draped it over his face. He leaned back, the cool outer rim of the tub jarring him like the hot water had.

Pilate breathed through the hot, damp cloth. Music from the clock radio in the adjoining bedroom crowded his ears. The CD was a mix of different tunes Pilate had made a few years ago; he'd uncovered it while unpacking and repacking some boxes before the move.

Carole King sang about "…following where I lead…" and Pilate found himself back in that drafty flat back home, his young bride singing along with her smoky British voice.

She was slicing celery for chicken salad, green slices as thin as parchment paper, and her hips moved with the music. Pilate saw his image in the shiny surface of the toaster on the counter, grinning. A skinny thirty-something married to a wild, sexy, foreign, exotic beauty, and there he was, grinning like an idiot.

Sam turned to face him, smiling her crooked smile, holding a knife with one hand and placing the other on her hip. "Honey, I have to go, so here." She thrust the knife between his ribs. She smiled and thrust it in twice more. Her eyes widened, her lips moistened by her pink tongue. She watched the blood flow out of Pilate as his astonished eyes rolled back in his head.

Darkness.

"And one to grow on." A voice not unlike Pilate's shattered the silence.

Though dead, Pilate snatched the washcloth from his face and looked at his torso. The skin was unbroken, the ribs intact.

In the candlelight of the hotel bathroom sat an old friend. Pilate had known him a long time—Pilate's conscience and insecurity given humanoid form. Pilate called him Simon, a name coined long ago, somewhat of a homage to the fictional thief Templar, the man who was so comfortable in the dark. This Simon talked with a voice similar to Pilate's, but he had a touch of the haughty, superior aristocrat in his accent for a reason Pilate had yet to determine. Simon perched on the toilet as if it were a true throne, lighting a cigarette.

"Damn it," Pilate said aloud, looking away, disgusted yet relieved.

"Well, hello to you too," he said brightly, as if Pilate had just greeted him on a cheery good morning.

Pilate looked back at him. As usual, Simon's shape was all he could make out, except for the occasional flicker of the glowing ember at the tip of the cigarette, illuminating his smooth, familiar face. What few snatches Pilate could glean from experience with the specter revealed a smoother, less human, but somehow more idealized version of himself. He couldn't be certain. "Ah damn it," Pilate said, dropping the washcloth in the water.

"Shh…listen…new song," Simon cooed, again puffing on a Dunhill.

It was Todd Rungren's "Hello, It's Me."

Pilate consciously prevented the song from triggering another memory and demanded coldly, "What do you want?"

"Oh, come on now," he said, again with his snooty singsong voice. *"Do allow me the fun of walking down Memory Lane with you again."*

"Why? So you can twist my memories into something ugly? Something vile?" Pilate sneered, his hand slapping the surface of the bathwater.

"But you always gain so much from what I have to show you," he said, sounding injured by the remark.

"I have come to the realization that you are nothing more than a byproduct of prescription medication, sir," Pilate said aloud, reaching for the small bar of oatmeal hotel soap.

Simon waved his arms above his head. The metallic clanging of chains and shackles thundered and echoed in the tiny lavatory. *"You may be a fragment of underdone potato or a crumb of cheese. There's more of gravy than of grave about you,"* he mocked. *"Booo!"*

"Oh, for Pete's sake," Pilate said.

"Maybe now we should go back to your wonderful, scene-chewing turn as young Scrooge in that dreadful community theatre."

"Just shut up" Pilate said, his eyes forward, staring at the dripping faucet. "And get on with whatever it is you want to say."

"Shut up or get on with it? Which will it be?"

The ash from the Dunhill made a ssst sound as it fell into the bath.

"For God's sakes, go on and get it over with," Pilate said, more demanding this time.

"Certainly."

"Thanks," Pilate said.

"I just figured your wife would be the last person on your mind this time of year…let's see, well, hmmm….maybe because her birthday was last month."

"Maybe it was just the song and that was it," Pilate said, playing along with Simon's little act.

"Any chance of you getting out of this bath? I am reminded of the French Revolution and The Artist Formerly Known As Prince, all in the same moment," Simon said, dropping the butt of the cigarette in the toilet.

"I am enjoying a hot bath, and I'm not getting out until I'm damn well ready to. So why don't you go away and let me have some peace?"

Simon waved away the comment as if it was the buzzing of a bothersome insect. *"No, no, I can wait. The sight of you sitting in there, wrinkling up like a prune isn't so bad. I can bear it."*

"How nice."

"How are you feeling? Your concentration will be very important now that you have a job again, you know. Can't leave yourself open to… what was the word? Layoffs. Like at the newspaper.

Oh, and I see you haven't taken your special vitamins lately, you naughty, careless boy. How long will it take you to fuck up this job without popping your pills like an obedient little drone?"

Pilate sat there, soaking and seething, stony silent.

Simon sighed. *"I'm afraid I can't wait after all, especially if you are not going to participate in this little conversation of ours. I haven't much time, so I'll get to the point. Something is going on in that head of yours to make you think more than a passing moment about the limey ex, and truthfully, I was shocked to see it was a sweet memory, until I edited it and made it more interesting,"* he said.

"You know, I'm trying to get to a point in my life where I can think about Sam with something less than contempt, and you have to come along and ruin it."

"Sorry to disappoint you, but I am only showing you what's in your heart, as always. Whenever you think of her in a kind way, a loving way, you have to make it bad in the end. If you don't, you'll never get over that fear."

"What fear?"

"That fear that keeps you running away. The fear that has you driving hundreds of miles to a new life—a new chapter, I believe you told that dealer—in a horrible little town. The fear that keeps you hiding out

from your logical path," he said in a mocking, pitying tone that made Pilate want to hold him under the bathwater and drown him.

"Just shut the hell up, would you?"

"Well, for once, it is not me who needs to shut up, it's you. You have just about talked yourself into trying again." Simon chuckled as if it was the most ridiculous notion he'd ever heard.

Pilate looked at his shadowy features. He was somehow not nearly as formidable-looking as he had been in the past. "Trying again? Is that wrong?"

Simon rose from the porcelain throne. *"No, as long as you can handle the consequences."*

"Consequences? Like finally meeting the right person and being happy?"

"Oh no." He moved the two steps from the commode to the tub quickly. *"The consequences are that the next time, you'll be left with only this."* His smooth hands grasped Pilate's head and pushed it underwater.

Surprised, Pilate choked on the warm, salty liquid that tasted of his own sweaty filth of the day. He thrashed at Simon's hands, clawing at him, but Simon's arms felt like wooden beams wrapped in steel cable. Amidst the thrashing, Pilate heard him laughing. When he did manage to rise out of the water for a second, his stinging eyes opened to an unbelievable sight: It was Samantha now, laughing and pushing him underwater again. Pilate let go and stopped resisting, and the pressure of the arms stopped pushing him down. His head lolled out of the water, his eyes red. "It...it wasn't supposed to end...to be like this," Pilate stammered, the words echoing off the tile.

CHAPTER FOUR

Cross College wasn't exactly a dump, Pilate decided, but it was damn close. He knew from his research about the school that the campus was the second oldest in the state. Firsthand he concluded it was neglected, like the redheaded, unwanted stepchild any school without a football program usually is in the American Midwest.

Pilate trudged around the campus for an hour or so after he arrived. He was too early to get his keys and the move-in paperwork for his faculty housing assignment, so he again gave in to his reinstated habit and fired up a smoke.

The old school had a standard oval layout, with eight buildings spread out like spokes from a once-proud library in the center. In front of the library, a state flag fluttered in the whipping winds under a tattered Old Glory. Most of the architecture was similar—circa 1910 or so—except for a disastrously ugly student center, a monument to the faux-optimistic *Fountainhead*-looking 1960s architecture that plagued so many institutions.

Patches of snow and ice dotted the oval. Numerous trees, all but a few stripped bare of their leaves by winter, were strategically placed alongside the cracked cement sidewalks. The occasional bench made pit stops around the diameter.

Pilate came across a bench with cracked slats that had a tarnished brass plaque on its back that read:

In Loving Memory of Dr. Gareth Kennedy

He took a seat on the rickety memorial and allowed his back to rest against the tarnished plaque. He sucked on the cigarette and squinted as the sun rose. *It's very quiet, this campus near the banks of the Missouri,* he surmised as he thought back to the events of the morning.

Early that morning, he'd crossed a steel bridge that spanned over the river. Once he'd crossed it, he had pulled his truck over to smoke. Floes of ice had rushed past the frozen mud banks, and the smoke from his cigarette had followed the current as he exhaled.

Pilate closed his eyes and wondered how he had come to be here, hundreds of miles from home…and from her. His thoughts traveled as well to the specter that had visited him last night in the casino hotel room.

He had wanted to take not just one but two of his antidepressants before he hit the road, hoping they would forbid Simon from coming and going as he pleased. Of course, he was unable to afford those little gatekeepers, so he had not taken any for the past two weeks or so. He wished at that moment that he had prevailed on his parents for enough money to at least buy the drugs.

A sudden real sense of being very small and vulnerable washed over him like the icy river. The same voice that told him he was a fake and worthless was now telling him he was exposed, in danger out there on the prairie.

He imagined Simon sharing the bench with him, mocking him with words like, *"But you have no support system here, no friends, not even cell phone service because this pathetic excuse for a town is too small and insignificant on the globe for a cellular tower."*

Pilate flicked his cigarette to the ground in disgust and frustration.

"Hey! Pick that up, mister."

Pilate's head jerked to his left, where he saw a clean-shaven, balding man of average height in his late fifties, clad in an elegant brown trench coat, striding very quickly toward him like a man on a mission. "Hmm?" Pilate said.

"I said pick up that cigarette," he admonished. "This is a college, not a damned ashtray."

"Oh, sorry." Pilate looked down and picked up the butt.

By now the man was standing over him. "Are you a student here?"

"Um, no," Pilate answered, suddenly feeling like a teenager who'd been caught with an illicit beer or a joint or making out with the preacher's daughter in the back seat of a car.

"What business do you have here?" he had an authoritative, even menacing quality. His eyes were dark, cold, and resolute. In less than a minute he had firmly established an asshole vibe, that was for sure.

Pilate stood. "I *work* here," he said, summoning his dignity. "Who are you?"

The man's eyes closed into doubting slits. "Name's Lindstrom. I'm no one special, just the school president." His voice barely concealed his glee at Pilate's faux pas. "Seems to me I ought to know who works for me…and who doesn't."

"Oh, Dr. Lindstrom! I'm sorry. I'm a new in—"

"Oh." Lindstrom glared at Pilate. "You're one of Trevathan's new replacements, huh?" He looked Pilate up and down. "That explains it."

"I just got to town, sir. I'm waiting for the Ad building to open so I can get my apartment keys." *Assuming I'm not fired,* Pilate thought.

"The building opens at eight," Lindstrom said. "I'd appreciate it if you were tidier about your smoking. This campus has enough blight. Don't need trash everywhere. Smoking's a nasty habit anyway, you know—for you and everyone around you who has to inhale that garbage."

"Yes, sir," Pilate said. He felt his ears reddening with embarrassment. "I, uh…I'm sorry if we got off on the wrong —"

By the time Pilate said "sir," Lindstrom had turned and walked away toward the Ad building. He did say something over his shoulder, and while Pilate couldn't be sure exactly what it was, he thought it sounded like, "That's one."

"Fucking hell," Pilate said under his breath, grasping the cigarette butt. *Can I screw up any worse? And I just fucking got here.*

Simon laughed behind Pilate's eyes.

Morgan Scovill looked down at the out-of-state license tag on the black Pontiac. The trunk was open, as was the door to the faculty apartment. Scovill spat out the cinnamon toothpick he'd been rolling around his mouth since after lunch. Approaching the door, he heard the alien notes of jazz. He leaned his head inside the door. "Anybody home?" he said. Something crashed to the floor in the small kitchen, and Scovill stopped inside the doorway as Pilate came into view.

Pilate, wearing a stained, ripped Pink Floyd t-shirt, saw the six- two, 280-pound frame of Sheriff Morgan Scovill obliterating the doorway. The middle-aged peace officer's hand casually rested on the butt of his holstered Glock semi-automatic. "Uh… hi," Pilate said.

"Hello," Scovill said. His right eye seemed like it was on permanent squint and his left betrayed what could be good humor.

"Um…" Pilate looked at the sheriff's firearm, then the small stereo that blared Miles Davis's "So What." He turned the volume down. "Too loud?"

Scovill didn't move. "Nah. Just doing the welcome wagon thing, you know? What with ya being new here and all."

Pilate gestured at the couch that came with the apartment. "Care to sit?"

Scovill eyed the tattered sofa with his squint. "No thanks. Listen, name's Scovill. I'm sheriff around here."

"I see. John Pilate." He extended his hand.

Scovill took off his hat, revealing thinning sandy blond hair with silver strands that matched his neatly trimmed beard. In a move he'd done a thousand times, Scovill wiped away the nonexistent perspiration along the rim of the felt hat with two fingers. "Well, Dr. Pilate—" he began.

"Mister. I'm not a PhD, so it's just Mr. Pilate. Actually, John will do just fine, Sheriff," Pilate said, lowering his hand.

Scovill looked annoyed. "Okay then. Mr. Pilate let me just say welcome to Cross. Besides being your local sheriff, I'm de facto head of security of this campus. We run a quiet place here —not much in the way of partying or drugs—and we wanna keep it that way. We don't need any outsiders coming in here…" Trailing off, Scovill glanced at the poster-sized framed black and white photo of a nude woman reclining on a rock; it set on the floor beside a suitcase, awaiting John to decide which wall would be its fate. "Anyhoo, we don't need nobody coming around here giving anybody any wild and fantastic ideas. Let me remind you that faculty housing is for faculty only, no students. No special tutoring, if ya know what I mean," he said, placing air quotations in the right places. "There's to be no dinners, no parties, no nothin' with students here. You got that?"

"Um, okay," Pilate stammered, feeling like he'd been pulled over for speeding in a school zone while wearing a t-shirt that read, "I got some candy, little girl."

"You're a young man, and Lord knows a man has appetites, but be advised you cannot and will not satisfy any such urges with any of the students who attend school here."

"Sheriff, I can assure you I have no intention of—"

"Good. Road to hell and all. If you mind these simple rules, you and I'll get along just fine."

Pilate looked around at the open cardboard boxes, then back at Scovill. His squinty eye seemed to be scanning every inch of him, as if committing Pilate to memory or making a decision.

"Yup," Scovill said, turning on his boot heel. "See you around campus, Mr. Pilate."

Pilate stood motionless for a moment, then nodded.

Scovill poked his head back inside the door. "Oh, and a word to the wise."

"What's that?"

"Don't go throwing your cigarette butts on the ground around here, especially in front of the president. Pisses him off, and we sure as hell don't need that."

Pilate watched the sheriff walk out the door and through the breezeway and then get into his SUV.

"Bad cop. No doughnut."

Night fell, and Pilate had not yet ventured any further than his apartment. Though hungry, he was too tired to search for food in the wilds of Cross Township. He rustled through a box and found a half-eaten bag of Doritos and washed them down with a tepid, flat Coke. Outside, it was pitch black, and it was only seven o'clock.

He put on his coat and stepped onto the breezeway porch he shared with yet-unmet neighbors. Puffing on a cigarette, he leaned against the brick wall. He casually looked up as he exhaled, then gasped. Stars rioted in the sky. Thousands of pinpoints of light populated the heavens with twinkling indifference to his wonder. "My...God." Pilate said, taking it in. He'd never really had a chance to gaze at the stars without the light pollution haze of a much bigger city, and he was taken in by nature's spectacle. Pilate obsessively attempted to count the stars between puffs off his cigarette; after about forty he gave up.

He stretched and looked to the south, viewing the pale glow of the campus. There were no students scampering about just yet; they would arrive next week.

Pilate had another day before he had to report to work. Trevathan, the dean who'd hired him over the phone, was expecting him at lunch the next day.

He crushed out the cigarette on the side of the apartment, sparks hitting his fingers, then flicked the spent butt into a nearby snowdrift. "Oops."

He wanted to spend some more time admiring Mother Nature's little fireworks show, but it was chilly, and he had things to do. The stars would have to wait.

PILATE'S CROSS

CHAPTER FIVE

Pictures were hung, books shelved, clothes stowed, and everything situated. His television picked up the dorm cable channels, all twenty of them, including a hunting channel that featured local deer trackers striking bizarre poses with their bloodied, vacant-eyed kills, bragging about the number of points on the antlers the animals would never be able to use again. He also stumbled across a porn channel, apparently a bootlegged one. The audio was bad, but the important part—the video—was pretty good.

He tried out the shower, an ancient affair with cracked tile and lukewarm brownish-colored water. He had been warned by a blasé, lisping housing manager named Larry that the water in Cross was a "tad cloudy" at times, and now that he was seeing it for himself, he realized that little weather prediction was a tad sugarcoated. "Delightful," Pilate said, ruefully recalling the comparatively opulent bathroom of the casino hotel, which would have been perfect, if not for Simon's presence. He sighed, reminding himself that it could be worse.

Seconds later, a cockroach reclining on his toothbrush challenged that notion. Dropping the insect into the toilet and the toothbrush into the cardboard box he was using as a makeshift trashcan, Pilate swilled some mouthwash, dressed, and drove into town.

"Town," as it was euphemistically called, consisted of a small convenience store-sized grocery; a two-pump gas station with a messy, greasy repair bay staffed by even messier, greasier mechanics; a bank; a post office; a bar; and a brightly-painted greasy spoon cafe. A small clapboard house had been converted into a Veterans of Foreign Wars headquarters alongside an impecunious bait shop that boasted of sales on beer and night crawlers.

An old Chevy with a snow blade labored to clear drifts from the post office frontage as Pilate went inside to open a mailbox account.

The postmaster was a polite, fifty-something woman who asked him no questions about where he was from or what he was doing in Cross. She did have his box application form ready when he walked in, however.

Pilate smiled at the woman, eliciting a forced grin. *Bureaucrats are bureaucrats, no matter where you go,* he considered. He also found out that he could return his rented truck at the local gas station, known as Jimmy's. He decided he'd drive the truck back later and walk back home since it was only about a half-mile and would be a welcomed reprieve after driving all that way.

In the cramped grocery store, he maneuvered the narrow aisles with a small, squeaky-wheeled shopping cart; the left front wheel didn't make contact with the linoleum at all and just spun in a haphazard circle as he walked. He loaded the cart with a new toothbrush, canned soup, crackers, lunchmeat, bread, and other bachelor staples. His preferred angel hair pasta was absent, so he had to settle for thin spaghetti, and as an accompaniment to the exorbitant pasta feast, he selected a generic canned spaghetti sauce labeled "with meat" and some Parmesan cheese; it was the ghastly stuff in the familiar green canister, and it smelled like feet, but there wasn't a lot of fresh fromage from which to choose. Comfort food was the order of the day: 2 percent milk, Coke, Doritos, Oreos, cigarettes, and a lottery scratch card. Casino winnings in hand, Pilate splurged and added a small plastic bottle of vodka.

The single checkout lane was clerked by yet another polite woman in her fifties; Pilate surmised in a grossly unfair, superior way that she had never ventured out of the county. She took his money, handed him his change, and said, "Welcome to Cross, Mr. Pilate."

"Uh, how do you know who I am?" he asked, baffled since he'd paid cash.

She snorted. "You can't fart in this town without someone smelling it."

"I see," Pilate said. "Well, thanks. I'll be seeing you."

"Yup," she said with a smile.

Now the town knows I eat junk food, smoke Marlboro Ultra Lights, and chase cheap pasta with cheap vodka, Pilate thought as he loaded his car trunk. When he shut it, he was instantly startled by a young girl of about six, standing beside him.

"You dropped this, mister," she said, gleaming at him with large brown eyes and the sun glistening off her blonde locks as she held the lottery scratch-off up to him.

"Oh, thank you, young lady," Pilate said. "That's most kind of you."

"You're welcome," she said, turning away and running up the slushy sidewalk to a woman's side; the girl's mother was about thirty, with slightly darker hair, large eyes, and a wary, yet strangely disarming smile.

Pilate waved at the pair.

The woman smiled again with a little more enthusiasm and turned away. She wore a powder-blue ski jacket, a red scarf, and tight Levi's that hugged her in all the right places. Pilate decided she had quite a nice rear-end to complement her smile.

The nice-assed woman with the interesting smile took the child's hand and walked away, and he watched the pair as they disappeared behind the post office.

In his car, Pilate scratched the ticket. "Ha! I can't lose," he said, looking into the rearview mirror as he backed up his car and wondering what that two bucks could buy him in the tiny little grocery store.

The sinister face of Simon peered back at him from the mirror. *"Oh really?"* he mocked. *"Seems to me you've proven that theory wrong many times."*

Ignoring Simon's taunts, Pilate turned onto the red brick road. He returned the rented truck and trudged home, taking in the Americana. His evening was much like the first. The porno channel, accompanied by music from his stereo (which clearly had to be better than amateur movie scripts or cheesy porno music) served as a diversion as he puttered away, arranging items in his cramped living room. He enjoyed a hearty meal of spaghetti, accompanied by vodka and two cigarettes. Feeling almost lachrymose from the vodka and starchy meal, he dozed until eleven. He smoked again, ventured outside to count more stars, then tottered off to his twin-sized rented bed.

The morning was announced by the school carillon, which played "If I Were a Rich Man," from *Fiddler on the Roof.*

Pilate rolled over twice before he came to the agonizing realization that he had to get out of bed. Either his alarm clock had failed him or he had turned it off in his sleep, because it was already 10:35 a.m., and he was due in the dean's office at 11:00. "Shit!" he screamed at the digital red numbers that seemed to be mocking his misfortune.

He showered, dressed, and sprinted to campus. He found the arts and sciences hall and presented himself to the dean's secretary. She eyed him with either contempt or disappointment; he wasn't sure. It was at that point that Pilate realized he had not shaved and wasn't sporting the most wrinkle-free of clothing. Three-day beard growth, tousled hair (and not the sexy kind), and the appearance of generally not giving a damn was no way to meet his new boss, and he knew it. *Maybe I should tap ashes on his floor too.*

"John?" said a voice in an accent reminiscent of North Dakota.

Or is it Minnesota? Pilate tried to determine as he turned to face Dr. Peter Trevathan, who stood in the doorway. He wore a tweed jacket, bolo tie, close-cropped steel-gray hair, and a world- weary expression. His shiny glass eye gaped at the secretary, while his good eye took in Pilate's shabby appearance.

"Dr. Trevathan? A pleasure," said Pilate, extending his hand. For the third time since he'd arrived in Cross, John Pilate's offer of a handshake went ignored.

Trevathan grunted, obviously not impressed with the near tardiness or the lackluster get-up. "Follow me," he sighed.

PILATE'S CROSS

CHAPTER SIX

Trevathan warmed to Pilate a little, and one of the first things he did was gently warn him to "Stay clear of President Lindstrom for a while," and then he thanked him for coming so quickly. Next, he went over a few procedural details, then accompanied Pilate to lunch at the cafeteria. "We've had some, uh, quick exits recently," Trevathan said, drinking coffee washing down his two bites of sweet potato pie with a gulp of coffee. His glass eye continued to wander when he looked at Pilate.

"Oh?"

"Yeah." He cleared his throat and coughed, then ran a hand over his short, steel-gray hair. "Lindstrom has been on sort of a remodeling kick, so to speak."

"I see," Pilate said, now feeling even worse about his run-in with Lindstrom and the great butt-tossing fiasco. He pushed his half-eaten chef's salad away.

"He never forgets a slight, and once he gets it in his head that you're against him or not 100 percent on his team, you're truly and forever screwed," Trevathan said. "That said, don't worry. I think you'll get a pass on the cigarette thing, being new here."

"Sorry about that. I was tired from the drive, and—"

Trevathan looked up at the clock, interrupting Pilate's lame excuse. "Just be more aware in the future." He drummed his hands twice on the table and smirked, a pained expression that failed miserably to suggest mirth. "Come on. I'll show you your office."

Pilate's "office" was about the size of a large walk-in closet, part of a warren of six similar rooms down the hall from numerous old classrooms. An ancient desk with an old matchbook under one of the legs, along with a coffee-stained cloth chair, comprised his workstation. An institutional hard plastic chair for visitors adjoined the desk.

Pilate hauled a box of books and a few odds and ends over from his apartment after Trevathan gave him the keys and showed him how to use the e-mail system. He placed the books haphazardly on a small, scratched oak shelf that matched the desk in color and condition. On the side was a small metal tag that read "Property of Cross College." After placing a framed photo of his parents on the desk and wiping what appeared to be lipstick and makeup residue off his telephone, he called his parents collect.

His mother asked about his missing tonsils; his father asked if he was getting along with the new boss.

Oh yeah, Dad. Primo.

Pilate ended the call with a promise to call every Sunday. Then, he picked up the syllabus for his first class, scheduled to start that week, Introduction to Creative Writing. He grunted at the formulaic class structure and tired notes from the last instructor, who had the improbable name of Donna Reed. Great. I'm inhabiting Donna Reed's office, about to teach her course load. "It's a wonderful life," he said and then chuckled at his own lame joke.

"Yeah? See if you still feel that way after you've been here a while," said a husky female voice.

Pilate looked up and saw the pretty woman he'd seen at the grocery store, the one with the dirty blonde hair and unforgettable ass. Startled, Pilate rose to his feet. "Um…hi. I didn't know anyone was around." On closer inspection, he saw that the woman's face, with only traces of makeup evident, was pretty but tempered with what Pilate surmised as a more than passing acquaintance with sorrow. Her arms were loosely folded across her chest, which filled out a pale blue sweater that matched her eyes. "John Pilate," he said, extending a hand.

She took it, and finally, since the time he'd arrived, someone had accepted his handshake. "Nice to meet you, John Pilate," she said. "Welcome to our little slice of heaven."

Pilate paused a moment to ponder the encounter. Her soft hand felt natural, warm and somehow comforting in his.

"I'm Kate," she said, looking him in the eye. "Kate Nathaniel, English and library science."

"Oh yes, Kate," Pilate said, pretending he'd heard of her. "We've met, haven't we?"

She nodded. "I suppose you could call it that, though it wasn't a proper introduction. At the store. My daughter found your lucky ticket."

"Right, thanks. It was lucky," he said. "Perhaps I should split the winnings with her."

"Your winnings?" she said, sounding skeptical.

"Well, a fifty percent cut would be a whole whopping dollar."

Kate smiled. "I hear you're from down South," she said, her arms uncrossing, her hands sliding into the pockets of her tight Levi's.

"Yes, yes I am. I'm from—"

When he was interrupted by the ringing telephone, they both looked at it.

"I wonder who could be calling me," he said.

"One way to find out," she said. "Talk to you later." She waved with her fingers and walked out as Pilate reached for the phone.

It was Sheriff Scovill. "Mr. Pilate, we need you to move your car," he said. "We're finishing some demolition of a structure next door to your apartment. The trucks need your space for the day, if you don't mind."

"No, not at all," he said. "Sheriff, if you don't mind me asking, what are they tearing down?"

Scovill paused.

Pilate imagined the man taking a toothpick from his mouth like a guard straight out of *Cool Hand Luke.*

"It's the old Bernard house. Been vacant a long time. The college bought it last month, and President Lindstrom wants it gone," he said.

Pilate moved his car from the path of trucks and equipment as they demolished the white two-story home next door to his faculty apartment. He loitered a moment to observe the heavy equipment as it pulled down the wooden skin and frame of the shabby residence.

"Sad in a way," said a man who had, during the noise of demolition, sauntered up to Pilate unobserved.

"Huh?" Pilate said, startled. He turned and saw a disheveled tie, sweater, baggy pants, and moth-eaten overcoat wearing a gangly man with prematurely gray hair. "Sad? How so?"

"Well, that house has to go, I guess, but there is so much history tied up in the old place," he said.

"Really?" Pilate said.

The man extended a hand. "Yes. I'm Derek Krall, school librarian and amateur town historian."

"Oh. Well, it's nice to meet you. I'm—"

"John Pilate, our smokin' new instructor," Krall said, smiling.

Pilate rolled his eyes. "Crap. Has everyone heard that story?"

"You'll soon find you can't fart around here without someone smelling it across town," he said with a wry chuckle. "How the hell did you end up out here in the middle of nowhere? If you don't mind my saying so, you don't look, uh…the type."

"Oh, you know—the usual series of missteps," Pilate said, smiling. "Man plans, God laughs."

"I hear ya," Krall said.

"So what big history is tied to this place?" Pilate jerked a thumb at the crumbling walls.

"The Bernard place? Where do I start?" Krall's eyes widened. He clearly loved the stuff, whatever it was. "That is —alas *was*— the scene of the most famous suicide in the history of this town."

"Oh," Pilate said, though he was surprised a self-homicide even stood out. Pilate frankly couldn't see much argument against suicide in the desolate winters of this burg. "Someone name Bernard offed himself?"

"Yup. Bullet to the brain." Krall put his finger to his temple and made a crude *bang* sound. "He was a professor too."

"That's encouraging," Pilate said, shrugging in his overcoat against a cold gust.

A monotonous *beep* issued from one of the heavy loaders as it backed up with a full load of debris.

Krall looked down at his feet for a moment, then at Pilate. "Yes, well, it's pretty extraordinary, considering."

"How so? Did he go psycho from the lonely winters here? Mentally ill?" Pilate realized the cold gust he felt was not a breeze at all; it was his old friend Simon. He saw Simon over Krall's shoulder, glaring at Pilate from the window of his apartment.

"Well, maybe. He sucked a bullet out of the barrel of a gun after he murdered his boss and the college president," Krall said.

"Oh, I see," Pilate said, his gaze torn away from the window and back to Krall's face from the grim account. "Tell me more."

Pilate followed Krall back to his cramped and, Pilate thought, laughably stereotypically messy office. Stacks of papers, dozens of school annuals, and what had to be at least fifty Post-it notes littered the large oak desk that ate up most of the room.

"Sorry for the mess," Krall said, bursting into a humorless staccato laugh. He bent over a filing cabinet and pulled out a large brown envelope, the kind you might use to mail a manuscript or magazines. When he offered it to Pilate, John saw label scrawled haphazardly in black marker across the top: "Assassination File: November 1963."

"Uh, thanks, but I went through my JFK conspiracy phase after the movie," Pilate said, offering a polite smile. "The Cross College incident, remember?"

Krall looked pained. "That's what this is," he said, leaving the "*moron*" unsaid.

"Sorry. November 1963, huh?"

"Yeah. It happened just a few days after President Kennedy was assassinated. Cross College lost its president to an assassin too. Ironically—or maybe not—Kennedy was the name of the dean killed along with the president."

Pilate found that interesting detail almost as weird as all those Lincoln-Kennedy assassination coincidences that had fascinated him as a child. *Lincoln had an assistant named Kennedy who warned him not to go to the theatre. Kennedy had an assistant named Lincoln who warned him not to go to Dallas. Pilate had a figment of his imagination that warned him not to go to Cross.*

Pilate opened the envelope. Inside were at least 100 pages of documents, photocopies, newspaper clippings, and graphic crime scene photos of the double murder-homicide. Aesthetically speaking, the one saving grace was that the grotesque images were not in color. One showed an almost comically surprised-looking President Keillor, his right eye a ghastly black hole, sprawled in his chair; another showed Kennedy, his puppet strings cut, a third eye bored in his forehead. Pilate flipped through a dozen or so other photos showing different angles of the same horrors. When he came to one of a portly man lying on a hooked rug, his arms extended like a tweedy Christ, a gun loosely spilling from one hand, he held it up to Krall, who had watched Pilate take in the gory photos wordlessly. "This Bernard?"

Krall nodded.

Another photo showed a close-up of Bernard's face, a crease where his glasses pinched his nose still apparent, his mouth a trickle of blood. A garish mosaic of dark, inky blood and brains oozed out from behind his head.

"God this is awful," Pilate finally said, thumbing back through the photos.

"Yes, it was."

"Humph. Why?" Pilate said, looking up a moment at Krall, who had his feet on his desk. "Why would somebody do this?"

"Well, he left a note." He dropped his feet to the floor, leaned over, and pointed to the photo, where a typed letter and fountain pen lay beside the body. "See?"

Pilate nodded.

"He left instructions for his burial, along with a postscript." Krall smiled, sat back down, and raised his eyebrows mischievously, clearly relishing the opportunity to tell the tale to a new listener.

"And?" Pilate prompted.

Krall gestured toward the envelope. "Gimme."

Pilate handed the packet back to him.

Krall fished through the papers until he found a copy of the letter, then handed it to Pilate. "Here's what the police transcribed from the original letter. Not sure where the actual letter is— probably lost in a box or hole somewhere."

Pilate took it, glanced at it, and immediately asked, "Who was Dr. Benton?"

"Hmm? Oh, the guy he asked to look after his affairs? He was a prof here, one of the few who could stand the guy."

"I see. So Bernard was..." Pilate was going to say "*misfit*" or "*loner,*" until he read the postscript:

P.S. *Wally tried to fire the wrong person.*

"Wally?"

"Dr. Walker Keillor. Nobody but his missus called him Wally to his face, and personally, I think Bernard meant it disparagingly. Walker had told Bernard a few days earlier that Dean Kennedy had agreed it was time for Bernard to move on," Krall said, putting his feet back up and laying the file on his desk.

"Oh. So they fired him?"

"Yes, as people sometimes do in academia. They just declined to re-up his contract...after twenty-four years." Krall whistled, making the sound of a bomb dropping, holding his hands behind his head to support himself while he leaned back. "Real bummer."

"Yeah, apparently so." Pilate chewed on his fingernail. "Sounds like the most interesting thing that's ever happened here." "Maybe," Krall said, "though I hear the flood of '43 was a pretty big deal."

Pilate spent a restless couple of days leading to New Year's, fighting the urge to go back home for the holiday. He had no money to make the trip, though, so he was forced to ring in the New Year in a rather lonesome fashion amidst a freshly fallen foot of snow.

He walked to the town bar on New Year's Eve. As gregarious as he liked to think he could be, he was nervous. The numerous pickups, Jeeps, and SUVs out front, coupled with the honky-tonk laughter from within, put him off. Pilate lit a cigarette with slightly trembling hands. As he glanced up, clouds obscured the wondrous blanket of pinpoints that had so moved him during his first few nights in town. He puffed on the smoke, still debating as to whether to go inside or go home. Snow started to fall again, and Pilate was startled by the sound of vehicle ignition and the glare of the floodlights from the sheriff's truck hidden in an alley across the street. Pilate gave a brief wave to the sheriff, though he did not notice any effort from the sheriff to acknowledge him. "Well shit," Pilate muttered. *Busted.* He couldn't just toddle home without going in.

He opened the bar door and was blasted by the music and laughter of the revelers. Pilate edged his way through the crowd that jammed into every bit of space. He recognized some of the regulars from the college: a toothless janitor, a couple of grizzled groundskeepers, and the de rigueur art professor with the gray ponytail and granny glasses. To his surprise, he also spied Dean Trevathan among the throng.

Trevathan was holding court with a couple of the groundskeepers and the plump short order cook from the college's fast-food style café. They sat around a small table, boilermakers parked in front of them, Trevathan's mirthless glass eye wandering as he gestured and spoke.

Suddenly, Pilate felt a painful blow to his right side, where a very large man with a party hat on his round head had bumped into him at full force.

"Sorry, friend," the man said, though the word "friend" seemed like it wanted to come out as "*asshole.*"

"Beg pardon," Pilate said, reflexive of many such accidental meetings in more bars, clubs, and discos than he could count.

"What did you say?" the man said, though he was so drunk it sounded more like "*Whadyusay?*"

"I said I beg your pardon," Pilate said, turning to order his drink.

The large man's face became very red; his piggy eyes bored into Pilate. "No, I beg *your* pardon, dickhead," he said, poking Pilate hard in the chest, spilling his beer down Pilate's leg.

Like most people, Pilate didn't like to be pushed, but he checked his first response, which was to push back; he was in a very bad place to look for backup. He held his hands up, as if he surrendered, and tried to back away from the man.

Backing away, however caused him to inadvertently place his Size 12 hiking boots on the feet of another man's date.

"Ouch! Get off!" the woman cried.

The woman's date shoved Pilate directly into the large man with the party hat.

Pilate felt the man's flabby belly give a little and heard him make an *oomph* sound. "Sorry, I—"

Pilate's sentence was rudely interrupted by the large man's fist smashing into his teeth, and in that second of shock, pain, and surprise the room became very bright, then very dark.

He awoke in the back of the sheriff's SUV and overheard Scovill talking to someone.

"I saw the whole goddamned thing, Scovill," it was Dean Trevathan, a tad drunk. "John Pilate was minding his own business when Haystack Calhoun slugged him."

Scovill's voice broke through the blackness, and Pilate opened his eyes. He saw Trevathan weaving a little as he stood beside the driver's side window, barking at Scovill.

"I'm sure you're right. Look, I'll make sure he's all right and take him home, okay, Doc?"

"Well, uh...you sure he doesn't need a doctor?" Trevathan said. "Naw. It's just a bruised jaw," Scovill said.

"What are you going to do about Craig Olafson?" There was a pause.

"Oh," Trevathan said. "The usual, huh? Not a goddamned thing." Pilate sat up and saw the dean stagger back to the bar.

Scovill farted loudly in the front seat.

"Man," Pilate moaned. "Not sure what's worse, my jaw or that fart, Sheriff."

"Count your blessings," Scovill said. "It coulda been a lot worse for you tonight."

"You mean it could *smell* worse? I seriously doubt that. I bet they really can smell that one across town." Pilate looked at Scovill's half-closed eye through the rearview mirror and took note of his expressionless face.

"I mean that guy could have put you in the hospital if Trevathan hadn't run out here to get me," he said.

"Sheriff," Pilate said, rubbing his jaw, "I didn't provoke that guy on purpose. I just—"

"No doubt," he said as he finally developed a facial expression. Pilate thought it was one of understanding, but the inscrutable sheriff was tough to read.

"Well, am I—"

"Free to go?" Scovill said, his eyebrow raised.

Pilate nodded.

"You handcuffed?" Scovill said.

"No."

"You pressing charges?"

"Should I?"

"Not if you plan to stay in Cross for any length of time," Scovill said.

"In that case, take me home, James." Pilate fell back into the ripped upholstery of the sheriff's truck and glanced at his watch. "Shit! That guy knocked me right into next year."

PILATE'S CROSS

CHAPTER SEVEN

Pilate's jaw was purple on New Year's Day. His doorbell rang just after eight a.m., as he gingerly touched a mug of coffee to his lips.

He gathered his bathrobe around him and answered the door.

"You all right?" Trevathan asked as Pilate opened the door and beckoned him inside.

"Uh, yeah," he said. "Dr. Trevathan, I want to assure you that I did nothing to provoke—"

"I know that. Craig Olafson is a fat-assed punk, a bully," Trevathan said, accepting a mug of coffee from Pilate.

"Why me though?" Pilate said, settling into his armchair.

"Why not you?" Trevathan snorted. "Makes no difference to his crowd. He's the mayor's kid, a lazy fat fuck who does whatever he damn well pleases in this town because of who his daddy is."

"I just keep making powerful friends here, don't I?" Pilate said. "Look, the good news is that President Lindstrom is out of town for a couple of days," Trevathan said. "The bad news is that he will hear about this. Strike two." "Strike two?"

"The smoking thing."

"You're kidding me! That was a strike?" Pilate set his coffee cup down.

"Mr. Pilate, Jack Lindstrom fired a groundskeeper for throwing a candy wrapper out of his truck *off* campus, downtown," Trevathan said. "The dumb-ass did it in front of Lindstrom just to antagonize him. Lindstrom's a real prissy bastard anyway. Of course, that's not the reason he gave when he fired the guy, but the guy is gone just the same."

"Great," Pilate said, his head in his hands. "Just great."

"Just lay low," Trevathan said, standing. "Glad you're okay, but my advice is to just go in, do your job well, and stay out of trouble. Hopefully that jaw will look better before the boss gets back, so it won't have him asking too many questions."

Pilate snorted at Trevathan's hangdog repeat of that phrase. "Well, what about you? Don't you care what he thinks of you?"

"I have tenure. That means I don't give two shits what Jack thinks of me." He chuckled mirthlessly. "I'm only interim dean, so I'm technically not management."

"What happened to the last dean?" Trevathan smiled.

"Great." Pilate showed the old professor to the door.

"Thanks, Doc."

"Yup." Trevathan trudged through new snow to his old pickup.

Pilate dozed that afternoon; he dreamt about the old murders and his new enemies. The school's carillon, from its perch in the tower over the library, played a tune he couldn't quite make out.

His jaw ached. He dug some Tylenol out of one of the cardboard moving boxes and took three, then finished his coffee and showered.

The water was the color of rust and not very warm. He hopped out, dried his hair with a towel, shaved under his chin and neck, and dressed himself.

Once he was much more presentable than the day he'd first arrived, he looked over the syllabi for his classes. Yawning, he put them aside.

Pilate unpacked some boxes of books and placed them in the built-in shelves on one wall of his new digs. One book, a gift from his grandfather, caught his eye: *Modern Criminal Investigation.*

His grandfather, a crime-novel-loving, would-be potboiler writer, had the book in his effects when he died. No one else much cared to have anything of his grandfather's, since none of it was worth much monetary value, but young Johnny Pilate had kept that book, and he cherished every underlined passage, every pencil-marked note his grandfather had left in the margin. There was something comforting in knowing that one day, his grandfather had tread across those very same words on those very same pages; he had been there, and John could revisit anytime he wanted.

Flipping through the index, Pilate searched fruitlessly for information on crime scenes, murder-suicides in particular. When he realized there was not much there, he gently placed the book on the shelf, treating the legacy with care.

After a boring night icing his jaw and availing himself of the pirated porn on television, Pilate awoke to the last day before semester office hours were to begin. He walked over to his office early.

The sunlight glared off the crunchy snow. He fished in his pocket for scratched sunglasses and slipped them over his bruised face.

The main door of the building was unlocked. He noticed some galoshes in the small entryway and some melting snow tracks leading to the dean's office up the hall. Pilate went the opposite direction, taking the stairs to the suite of closets, one of which was his office.

At his office door was a fat manila envelope. He had just picked it up and started to open it when he noticed that Kate Nathaniel's door was open. Pilate slipped the envelope under his arm and walked over to Kate's door. He poked his head in and was treated to a nice view: Kate on all fours, under her desk, plugging in her computer. Sting's "Fields of Gold" played on the radio as a fitting backdrop for the occasion. "Hi," Pilate said, his eyes helplessly drawn to her Levi's-clad ass.

As predictably as a character in a television sitcom, Kate bumped her head in surprise. "Shit!" she said. She crawled out from under her desk, her hand clamped to the crown of her head, glaring at Pilate in annoyance.

"Sorry," he said, stifling a laugh.

"No problem," she said, her face softening as she rose to her feet. "Well, well. If it isn't Rocky Balboa."

Pilate rolled his eyes upward, turning his bruised jaw away from her. "Geez. Word travels fast around here."

"It has been said that you can't fart in Cross without someone smelling it across town," Kate said.

"That's a new one," Pilate fibbed, leaning against the doorjamb. "I just got on the wrong side of a Mack truck."

"That's a new one," Kate also fibbed, sitting in the wheeled chair beside her desk, flicking on the computer monitor.

"Heh. Yeah."

"So," she said, fishing in her desk drawer for a rubber band, "you ready to stop your brawling and start teaching?" Her eyes smiled, and she had her hair back in a way that reminded Pilate of a cheerleader he had kissed in high school.

"Hell yes." Pilate shifted his weight from one foot to another. "I'm ready for an invigorating semester here at Cross."

"Sounds delightful. Thirteenth grade? High school with ashtrays?" Kate touched the tip of her nose with her finger and pointed at Pilate. "Lindstrom has pretensions of making the place some sort of 'Harvard of the Midwest,' but most people are pretty dubious."

"How long you been here?"

Kate's eyes glanced at a framed photo on her desk, the subject of which he could not see. "Six years."

"And I suspect you've had enough," he said.

"You suspect correctly."

"So why stay?"

"Criminal record. Bank robbery." She smiled. "I didn't want to get too far from home," she said.

"Oh, so you're a native?"

"No, but my husband is," she said.

"Oh, I see," Pilate said, feeling foolish. He had not noticed a ring previously, and he clumsily and quite obviously looked to see that there was no ring now.

"Gone," she said, coolly but not unkindly, as if she had said it enough times with the required feeling. "Passed away."

"I'm sorry to hear that," he said.

"Thanks. Anyway, I don't want to take Kara too far from her grandpa. He lives in the next town over," she said. "He owns the mortuary or funeral home or whatever you want to call it."

"I see," Pilate said.

There was a pause; Donald Fagen's "I.G.Y." filled the void. "Well, I better get to work on my grade book," Kate said, her ponytail bobbing as she turned her head to the computer screen and back to Pilate.

"Me too," he said, turning away from her door and pointing to his office. "Nice talking with you."

"You too, bruiser. Keep your left up."

Settling into his office, Pilate turned on his computer and set the manila envelope aside while he brewed some coffee in the office anteroom. He heard Kate singing along to the radio a little.

When he sat back down at his desk to wait for the coffee to brew, he opened the envelope marked "John Pilate" and emptied it on his desk. Neat photocopies of crime scene photos, witness affidavits, and news clippings from the murder-suicide spilled out. A Post-it note on the police report from 1963 said simply:

I could tell you were interested. Enjoy!

Krall

Pilate didn't get around to opening his grade book that morning.

CHAPTER EIGHT

The first week of school was the usual array of new students, all asking, "Will this be on the test?" seemingly every other moment in his lectures. Thick-waisted farm girls with too much makeup and very little academic interest pranced before the watchful eyes of young men with sex, cheap beer, and not much else occupying their minds. Pilate decided Kate's appraisal of the studentry was very close to on target.

That wasn't to say there weren't some bright spots beyond the girls with tight sweat pants featuring sex kitten phrases on their asses. There were a few students in every class who clearly viewed college as an opportunity to escape the rustic hell where they'd grown up, and Pilate aimed to help them as best he could.

The morning's speech class was entertaining. He had assigned a five-minute speech, "about something you feel strongly about." Pilate guiltily took some sick pleasure in counting how many times students said "uh, like, and you know" in their speeches about smoking, Jesus Christ as their personal savior, their housecats, and even their cars. That depressing output aside, Pilate's elitist bias against the mostly rural students was challenged by a few standouts.

One such student was a popular senior basketball player named Riley Pierson, who exploded the stereotype of the big man on relatively small campus. Riley was a good-looking, intelligent, pleasant kid. His folks owned a grain elevator in Goss City. Pilate had no illusions that Riley wasn't a hell-raiser, but he seemed to balance it pretty well.

Riley's first speech in class was a bold talk about why it was important for Cross College to become more sensitive to the handful of foreign and minority students enrolled there. He related an incident that had occurred in his first semester, when two black basketball team members recruited from Kansas City had quit the team and left Cross. Excellent players, each topping six-five, the players were called "The Twin Towers." The Towers quit Cross, Riley said, because someone slid *Little Black Sambo* children's books under their dorm room doors with cryptic threats scrawled in the margins. "We could've gone to regionals that year if people here hadn't run Terrell and Anthony off," Riley said. "Cross College needs to know that racism hurts us all. We're all on the same team. Think about it."

Though Pilate could argue that the net effects of the racist acts were more far reaching than losing a basketball tournament, he had to give Riley credit for talking about such a volatile topic. From the nods of fellow students and a couple of dreamy stares from girls, Pilate felt Riley's talk had resonated.

After class, Pilate ran into Krall in the cafeteria and thanked him for the "reading material."

Krall invited Pilate to join him. As they dug into their lunches—the school had a remarkably good salad bar and grill — Krall surveyed the room. "Well, I figured you'd need something to occupy your mind during these cold winter nights when you aren't grading papers," he said.

"Yeah, thanks," Pilate said, spearing a sliced hardboiled egg on his salad. "The amateur porn hour is only so entertaining."

Krall leered over his tray. "Well..." He gestured with his fork at a table of hard-bodied, arguably pretty students. "There's always the extracurricular. You like volleyball?"

Pilate laughed. "No thanks. Even if it wasn't a no-no, I don't need the aggravation."

"Aggravation? What's aggravating about fucking a nineteen- year-old coed?" he said, smiling.

"Roughly everything leading up to and everything after it," Pilate said.

Krall laughed a little too loudly and cleared his throat. "True. There're always chat rooms, you know. That's fun. You have your home Internet set up yet?"

"Nope. Can't afford it yet," Pilate said.

"Didn't those idiots tell you that you get a free hookup to the college's backbone?" He snorted when Pilate shook his head. "Assholes. Look, go over to IT Services in the library and get a wireless card for your laptop. They'll give you a password, and you'll be surfing in no time."

"Thanks. That's great," Pilate said. "It'll be helpful."

Both chewed their food for a moment, Pilate discreetly surveyed the potential aggravations milling about the cafeteria.

"There're other interests around here for a young man like you—interests of the non-student variety," he said.

Pilate made a dismissive gesture.

Krall leaned forward again over his tray. "Your officemate, Kate, could probably use a good warming up on these cold winter nights," he leered.

Pilate tried to chuckle nonchalantly.

Krall continued to look at Pilate in his odd, wide-eyed manner, then leaned back in his chair, making a retreating gesture with his hands.

President Lindstrom walked into the cafeteria. He wore a fancy barn coat with a maroon scarf tied like an ascot around his neck; his scalp was shiny through thinning hair. He nodded at a few people he walked past and went ahead of several students and staff to the front of the food line.

"Prissy" was Trevathan's word.

"So what's her story?" Pilate said.

"Who, Kate?" Krall cackled, clapping his hands. "I knew it!" Pilate watched Krall enjoy his victory and ate more salad.

Krall wiped his mouth. "Well, our Katie is the town's most eligible widow. As you have already discerned, she is easy on the eyes and very sharp, but that woman can be a little standoffish. I think she needs a good, hard—"

Pilate's eyes darted to Krall's, stopping him from finishing the sentence, though there was no stopping the thought.

Krall cleared his throat. "She came here about five or six years ago when she married Grif Nathaniel's son Rick, straight out of college. Grif runs the mortuary next town over. Some people call him 'Grief'—nice nickname for a mortician."

"How droll. What happened to her husband, to this Rick?"

Krall grinned a little, but for his own peace of mind, Pilate decided it had to be more of a grimace. "He got clobbered by a grain truck a couple years ago. He was out driving a hearse with a stiff in it, and that grain truck barreled out into the road off one of those dirt field roads. By the way, be careful after harvest, man. Those guys have killed more than a few students in those kinds of accidents."

Pilate set his burger on the plate as Krall continued.

"Sheriff Scovill—I know you've met him… Oh, how's your jaw, by the way?"

Pilate glared.

Krall cleared his throat.

"Anyway, Scovill found Rick pinned in the hearse, ground up under the wheels of that truck. The stiff in the back had flown from the back into the front seat area with Rick. The body wasn't in a bag, and the sheet came off during the collision. Our heroic, esteemed sheriff saw it and thought the stiff was riding shotgun with Rick."

"Damn," Pilate said.

The clatter of trays in the dish return began to grow louder as students returned to classes and dorms.

"Yeah. Scovill said Rick was alive when he got there, that Rick was trying to tell him something." Krall's gaze clouded over, as if he were recalling something he'd actually lived through or been there to witness. "Something about the Missouri."

"The river?" Pilate said.

"No idea. Scovill couldn't make it out. Said Rick choked out a few odd things about the river and then some 'tell Kate and Kara I love them' kinda stuff. Poor fella bled out on the spot, with that stiff corpse sitting right next to him. Scovill tried to revive him. Hell, Scovill tried to revive the corpse until he figured out there was no point."

"Shit," Pilate said. He observed President Lindstrom carrying a tray of food into the administrative dining room. Behind Lindstrom was, from what he could tell, an attractive man of about twenty-five, carrying Lindstrom's barn coat and opening the door for him. "That must have been so rough."

"Yes. It's how Rick's granddaddy, Martin Nathaniel, died too—except his ass went over the suspension bridge into the icy Missouri. That wasn't too long after the Bernard murders, as I recall."

"Whoa! That cool bridge? What are the odds of both father and son dying in car crashes."

Krall shrugged. "It is weird, huh? Anyway, our Katie has never really gotten over losing Rick, I suspect," Krall said. "Then again, who can blame her?"

"So she stays," Pilate said, sipping his Coke.

"Yeah. I guess Grief takes care of her and Kara," Krall said, polishing off his drink. "Of course, she got a lot of insurance money and holds Rick's shares of the family business for Kara, though she pretty well stays out of that. She's an adjunct instructor with just a couple sections to teach. I know she doesn't make a whole lot doing that. I think if she could get a good teaching job somewhere else, she'd probably take it. I mean, this place is just a reminder—and whenever she takes Kara to see her grandpa, it's over at the same damn mortuary where they made Rick presentable for his funeral."

"Jesus," Pilate said. "That's gotta suck."

"It does. You know, Grief's dad, Marty, was teaching him the trade when the Keillor-Kennedy murders happened. He assisted with the funerals." Krall burped.

Pilate's mind harked back to the murder-suicide information Krall had shared. "Why do you suppose he did it?" Pilate asked.

"Who, Bernard?" Krall cracked his knuckles. "Like you asked about before, I think the guy went nuts, especially after he found out they were going to fire him after all those years."

"That simple?" Pilate said.

"I think so," Krall said, "but it's a fascinating story nonetheless, and part of our town history, grim as it is. I figured it might be a nice introduction to this little town of ours for you."

"Yeah, thanks," Pilate said. "You know, there might be a good story in there somewhere—maybe a magazine article or even a book." "Yes, I was thinking the same thing. What do you suppose? Kind of a look at this horrific event and the effects it had on a town? You writers. Always looking for new ways to fill my shelves."

"Exactly," Pilate said.

"Just the thing to keep you busy in this boring little town on cold winter nights when you're sick of grading papers," Krall smiled and stood.

Pilate grinned. "Well, thanks for looking out for my entertainment."

"Don't mention it…and when you write about me, it's K-R-A-L-L." He laughed. "But I do got a word of advice for ya."

"And what's that?"

"Um, just don't publish it until you move on from here."

"Why not?"

"Isn't it obvious? Perhaps the fact that you'll embarrass the town by dredging up its pathetic Peyton Place murder story."

"Good point," Pilate said. "An exposé like that could drum up some publicity our ambitious college president would like to avoid, I suppose."

"Yes, our president, among others." He snickered as a buxom girl walked by wearing a Minnesota baseball jersey with the word "Twins" emblazoned across her chest. "Nice twins."

Pilate smiled and sighed.

"So anyway, lay low with that murder stuff. Save it for later, after you've moved on. Then you can make it into a steamy mystery novel with lots of hot coed sex. You can use that bootleg porn channel for inspiration, so jot down some notes while you're watching it." Krall picked up his tray and walked away. Over his shoulder he said, "Besides, you wouldn't want another strike against you, would you?"

The Lindstrom Renaissance: This was the unofficial name put to the $65 million capital campaign to bring rickety old Cross College kicking and screaming into the latter part of the twentieth century. A new science building, a new library, and enough fancy new computers to overwhelm Bill Gates were the main goals.

Pilate surfed the college website and clicked on the special section devoted to the campaign. Though he did harbor some personal distaste for the man, he had to admit that Lindstrom's plan was ambitious, bold, necessary, and smart.

Cross College was one of the oldest schools in the state, yet it had very rarely been given its fiscal due from the legislature. Lindstrom was the first president in twenty-five years who had the backing and the will to move the school beyond mere survival into rebirth and full-scale growth. From what Pilate could glean from campus scuttlebutt and a quick Web search, Lindstrom had made his appearance at Cross about two years prior, after an apparently stormy term as a foundation executive at a Jesuit school in Pennsylvania. The man's past was a tad sketchy: He counted failed novelist, noted professor of mathematics, and even insurance agent as past careers. Regardless of those broken career paths, Lindstrom really was good at raising money, and the days of academics leading small, financially troubled colleges like Cross were over. Now, it would take skilled politicians and talented public relations practitioners, fundraisers and friend-raisers. Bricks and mortar, elimination of deferred maintenance, and abolition of the tenure of lazy professors were high on the agenda.

Krall—who seemed to have the dirt on everybody at Cross and had no problem dishing it out to Pilate—had remarked that Lindstrom was "a ball breaker and a son of a bitch." Cross College had appointed a new board of trustees after a rare Democrat governor cleaned house a few years earlier, and that new board demanded that someone to either fix Cross College or drive a stake through its heart once and for all.

Lindstrom was married, but his wife kept to herself other than giving piano lessons to townie kids out of her station in the president's house. The closest person Lindstrom had to a confidant was the college's foundation director, Dick Shefler, who'd arrived at Cross a few years after he did. A sharp-tongued young man, reputedly with an eye on elected office, Shefler was the smooth yin to Lindstrom's brash yang. As Krall said, it was "not a bad combination when trying to squeeze contributions from complacent, rich alums."

Lindstrom had fired (or "strongly encouraged," as Krall emphasized) the retirement of more than eleven faculty and staff members during his short two years as president. He also had a history of ugly run-ins with students, parents, athletic teams, and boosters who failed to conform to his codes of behavior.

"Prude guy," Krall said. "He finds outward displays of humanity distasteful."

In the town, outside of the boundaries of the campus where he reigned, Lindstrom established himself as a game player: a no-regrets, kiss-my-ass carpetbagger and puppet master. When the town council refused his request to tear down a vacant, dilapidated house near the president's home, he and Shefler used college foundation funds to buy the house and renovate it into their newest faculty parking lot. He hosted a cookout for faculty, staff, and students on his lawn as the wrecking ball flew. Most recently, the cursed old Bernard place had been turned into kindling without a fight; there was no need to stage a midwinter cookout over that one. Lindstrom wasted little energy ingratiating himself to the townsfolk. They were the ants crossing his lawn, as far as he was concerned, and if they became too annoying, he just crushed their anthills.

Krall also divulged that Lindstrom was one of the few who did not fear Mayor Olafson. More than one person had overheard Lindstrom threatening Mayor Olafson's job. "He said something like 'Mayor, play ball or I'll get Dick Shefler to run against you, and he'll win. Then we will get things done,'" Krall said with glee.

"Did he do it?" Pilate asked. "I mean, there's no way he would win, is there?"

"Nah, unless Lindstrom could whip up the students to vote here in town for Shefler. That'd be a stretch, but it would've given Ollie some heartburn all the same. Anyway, it got the message across, and it was really ballsy." He knitted his brows together. "Actually foolhardy, though, now that I think about it," Krall said.

"How so?"

"Well, ya see, our man Olafson isn't like his daddy, who was mayor back when the Bernard murders happened. Old man Olafson woulda cut Jack's heart out for even speaking such a threat—or, at the very least, run him out of town on a rail. Our Mayor Olafson of today is a tad more, uh…civilized. He believes revenge is a dish best served cold or not at all."

"So the violent gene skips a generation?" Pilate said, thinking back to the mayor's son and his own bruised jaw on

New Year's Eve. "I wouldn't say that, but I would say the thoughtless violence gene does," Krall said, his eyes gone cold.

"Ollie will get Lindstrom one of these days. He's got home team advantage, and Lindstrom is dancing on a razor blade over a pool of lemonade. You just wait and see."

Pilate chewed that conversation over in his head a few times.

Lindstrom's apparently got some strikes against him too.

The phone rang in the midst of Pilate's placid remove of dreams. He risked opening an eyelid to check the time: three thirty a.m. Righteously pissed for at least two seconds, then instantly concerned—*It could be bad news from home*—Pilate groped for the phone. "Hello?" he said, sounding much sleepier than he thought he would.

"John?"

He knew the female voice, but in his half-lucidity, he couldn't place who it was. "What?" he said, shaking off the sleep.

"It's me, Sam."

Oh yeah. The British vowels. He sat up in bed as if a trumpet had announced the Lord's second coming. "Sam? What the hell?"

"I heard you were sick, and then I couldn't find you," she said.

"Sam, did you just leave the bar? Are you drunk?"

"For fuck's sake, of course I am," she said, exhaling the smoke from a Benson and Hedges. "Do you think I'd call you while I'm sober?"

"What do you want? And how did you find me?"

"I heard you have…cancer."

"Cancer? What the fuck are you talking about?" Pilate reached for his pack of cigarettes.

"You had throat surgery for cancer, didn't you? That's what I heard."

"Well…yes," he said, not exactly a lie. He lit his cigarette.

"Why didn't you call me?" She sounded genuinely pained. "Oh, I don't know, Sam. Perhaps I assumed you were too busy screwing the bartender you left me for."

There was silence for a moment, until Samantha coughed. "John, why did you leave?"

"Stupid question. Next?"

"I'm sorry, John."

A man's voice in the background called to Samantha. She hung up.

Pilate stubbed out the cigarette, threw the phone on the floor, and spent the next hour trying to get back to sleep, to no avail.

Against her best instincts, Kate Nathaniel had become John Pilate's friend. Over the course of the first three weeks of semester, she had broken down and joined him for lunch four times. Tonight, it was to be dinner. "Let's not eat here in Cross," she begged. "I don't need the gossip. Let's go over to Goss City. Besides, I have to pick up Kara at her grandfather's after dinner."

Goss City conjured images in Pilate's mind of buildings with more than three stories and modern conveniences the town of Cross could not offer. Thus, he was sorely disappointed.

It was readily apparent that Goss City was actually not a city by the strict definition. Goss City had been Cross's rival before the flood calamity and had added the word "city" to its name in the vain hope it would become a self-fulfilling prophecy. In a way, Goss did achieve those heights when the state highway was installed in the 1950s. At that point, the town became a way station for grain trucks, over-the-road supply trailers, and a minor farm equipment sales Mecca. Now, 3,422 people "and a few old soreheads" called Goss City home. It had a grocery store, dry cleaner, movie house, hardware store, several taverns, a decent prefab-metal bowling alley, Pierson's grain elevator, and good public schools. It was not really a city, but there was hope.

Kate recommended Sulky's Tavern for dinner. She described it as "dark and quiet, with huge steaks." It was the sort of place with kitschy shit nailed up all over the walls, but Pilate got the strong impression that Sulky's had been decorating that way long before the ubiquitous national chain restaurants had caught on to the trend that they tried to deny was a trend.

"Why do they call it Sulky's? Is that a proper name?" Pilate asked as they slid into a booth beneath a metal license plate and an ancient photograph of a ghostly looking woman with dark hair.

Kate smiled and shook her head, pointing to the picture hanging over the bar of a very sulky man indeed.

"I see. The founder?" Pilate said, smiling back at her.

She nodded.

They ate chicken fried steak, Sulky's specialty, and chased it with ice-cold beer. Pilate had very little taste for beer; especially in the wintertime, but he didn't want to order the hard stuff their first time out.

"How's your jaw?" Kate said.

"It was fine until I had to chew on this steak," Pilate said.

"Yeah, I guess it is a little rubbery," Kate said.

"Sorry."

"No problem."

An awkward pause was broken by small talk about the snow and ice, which Pilate learned had been rather light for that time of year, relative to what they usually had to contend with. The discussion moved on to work and students for a while, then reverted to silence.

"Do you like it here?" Kate said in the middle of the lull.

"Um, it has its charms," he said. "Nice people, good school." Kate looked askance.

Pilate exhaled a long sigh, pushing his half-finished leathery steak and baked potato away. "No, Kate. No, I really don't."

Her face brightened. "Thank God! For a minute there, I thought you were completely insane."

"But this is your home," he said.

"No." She put her fork down. "This was *Rick's* home."

"Well, it's gotta be tough for you to stick around here," Pilate acknowledged.

"It can be, yes, but Kara's near Grif, and that's important," Kate said, smiling and waving at a couple who walked past their table. "But Grif's wife Velma died a few years ago, and Kara's nearly school age. I want her to go to a decent school."

"I see. So you're planning on leaving?"

"If I can find work," she said, sipping her beer. "Besides, I don't think I fit in with Jack Lindstrom's new idea of Cross College."

Pilate laughed. "What makes you say that?"

"Oh, he has made some noise about getting rid of a lot of us adjuncts and using out-of-state teachers for Internet classes," she said.

"You could teach those," Pilate said. "I've done it."

"And did you find it half as challenging or interesting as being an instructor in person?"

"Touché," Pilate said. "However, I don't think I'll be in the teaching game for very long. I guess I don't have such a passion for it."

"Too many memories here, John," she said, ignoring his last statement. Her husky voice had a wistful quality for a moment, but then it was gone. "But anyway, I plan to finish the semester and watch Olafson and Lindstrom fight it out over the Bartley place."

"The Bartley place?" Pilate asked.

"Yeah. You haven't you heard about that? It's the huge farm on the outskirts of town. Ollie and all his Klansmen pals are trying to keep Lindstrom from buying it for the college.

They want to put up a strip mall adjoining the highway and maybe a golf course—a nine-holer, I think."

"What's Lindstrom want it for?"

"He thinks he'll need it for dorms for all the hundreds of new students his fancy new marketing guy is going to bring in."

"Oh right. That guy," Pilate said, thinking of the talented, high-priced marketing executive Krall had mentioned Lindstrom luring to campus.

"I hear he's very good looking," she said, smirking.

"And don't forget the Jack Lindstrom student union," she said. "I read the online prospectus for the capital campaign. I don't remember anything about a new student union."

"Oh. Well, Lindy thinks he's going to overshoot the capital campaign goal. Then he'll get Dick Shefler to say, 'Lookee here, folks! Good ol' President Jack did so well we should also build an Internet tech center and name it after our dear leader.'" Kate's sarcasm was funny and surprising.

"You don't much like Jack, do you?"

"I have my reasons," she said, interrupted by the waitress with the check. She looked at her watch. "I need to go get Kara. Can you take me back now so I can get my car and get her."

"I can take you over there. No sense in you going all the way back home then here again," he said, laying money on the table.

"Well…" She looked up for a moment. "Okay, but we have to make sure Kara doesn't think we were doing anything."

Pilate smirked. "Like what?"

The Nathaniel Funeral Home had been in business for nearly a century, though the current structure had only been built atop the basement some twenty years ago after a freak tornado ripped off the roof. Pilate had learned from Krall that the twister had snatched three bodies out of the structure and deposited two naked corpses from the embalming room onto the front lawn of the county tax office.

The third body remained in its coffin and flew nearly a mile, landing right side up with the lid open in the middle of the Bartley cornfield. Local lore had it that not a hair on the corpse of Dorothy "Dottie" Mostek's head was out of place, and her hands remained clasped over her cancerous chest.

Just a few years ago, the structure had burned to the ground due to an unexplained fire. It was rebuilt again, right on the same spot.

Next door to the funeral home stood a lovely three-story Victorian manse, all white and gingerbread. A massive front porch hugged three sides of the first floor, complete with a porch swing.

A small Mercedes SUV pulled out of the drive as they entered, the headlights from Pilate's car revealing Jack Lindstrom's scowl.

"Isn't that...?" Pilate said.

"Oh, what does he want?" Kate said. "I've had enough of him sniffing around."

"What does he want?" Pilate said, parking the car.

"Lots of things he can't have, but I'm assuming this time, he wants Grif's help in getting the Bartley deal pushed through. Probably thinks Grif has dirt on Ollie. Let's not talk about him, okay?"

"Suits me," Pilate said, looking at Lindstrom's taillights disappear down the road.

"That's Grif's house," Kate said. "It's been in the family a long time."

"It's nice," Pilate said. He nodded at the mortuary. "And I guess that's where the family business works?"

Kate nodded at the obvious statement. "Let's get Kara. Come on."

It was dark, though a partial moon glowed over the trees that stood sentry over the cornfields behind the house and mortuary.

They hurried the way cold people do in winter, up to the solid wooden porch and into the house. Kate did not knock, instead sweeping in with Pilate in tow. He closed the screen and main doors to avoid letting the cold in.

"Grif? Kara?" Kate called, loosening her scarf.

The room was a study in formality—replete with doilies covering the backs of Victorian furniture; elegant coffee and end tables matched the settee and wingback side chairs. A fireplace dominated the room; its mantle held a large pewter urn bracketed by silver framed photos of family members.

"This house used to be the actual funeral parlor, as they called it. That was a long time ago—turn of the century," she said. "They built the place next door—well, actually the basement is all that's left of that one. A fire wiped it out a few years ago. Your buddy Krall can probably tell you all you want to know about it. He seems to be the town historian these days."

"He actually mentioned a bizarre tornado too."

"Oh right. That was way before my time," she said, calling for them again. She waited a moment, sighed, and put her scarf back around her neck. "I'm sorry. They must be next door. He knows I don't want her over there."

"You mean at the—"

"Yes. I know there are emergencies sometimes, especially in his line of work, but I just don't like her over there in that atmosphere. She doesn't need to see corpses and crying families and all that stuff."

They walked through the spacious living room, past the staircase, to the kitchen. It was actually very modern when compared to the rest of the house. A stainless steel Subzero fridge, Blodgett oven and range, and a freestanding butcher block, complete with a set of expensive knives dominated the kitchen. The spotless countertops sported a matching blender and coffee grinder, with coffee and sugar canisters.

"Sometimes we help families prepare their reception meals after the funeral," Kate said, noticing Pilate's expression of interest in the kitchen. "Grif has a small reception hall over there. Lots of families use it and have food."

"I see."

They exited the back door to cross the thirty feet between the house and mortuary. Pilate saw a small icicle-draped playground for kids in the back, paint peeling off the bars, a birdbath with Saint Francis, and a massive stack of firewood. A chimney rose from the rear of the building.

"Oh, how nice. There's a fireplace in there too."

Kate snorted. "No, John. That's part of the crematorium."

"Oh." *God. Could I have said anything dumber?*

They entered through the very commercial-looking glass door of the mortuary. The mortuary "living room" consulting/waiting area was a pale, cheaper copy of the ancient one he'd just left in the Victorian house. A small office with Grif's name on the door was situated to the side.

"Not in his office. Could you wait here? I'll go see if I can find them," Kate said walking through a door marked "Private."

Two large paintings hung above a sofa in the living room. One was actually a photo of a handsome man in his twenties, wearing a navy-blue suit and elegant tie. A small brass plaque mounted on the frame read "Richard David Nathaniel 1974-2000." *Rick.* Kate had walked past the picture as if she had not seen it; a skill she'd no doubt worked hard to master.

Next to Rick's photo hung an older portrait of a distinguished-looking thin man in his fifties, wearing a pleasant, yet somber expression and black suit to match. Pilate noted the small brass plaque: "Martin Alexander Nathaniel 1917-1963."

A stack of brochures about prepaid funerals and some religious tracts lay untouched on the end table. One tract read, "Your Choice: Heaven or Hell!" and it featured an unintentionally comical drawing of Satan on the cover.

Pilate observed quickly that past Grif's office were a large casket showroom and four mourning rooms, all with the lights off. "Death takes a holiday," he said under his breath. Then he took in the room, thinking about the Nathaniel family. They had played a minor role in the Bernard tragedy all those years ago. Martin Nathaniel had been funeral director for all three of the men, and the man known as "Grief" had been apprentice. Pilate found it strange that Martin Nathaniel's car had plunged over the bridge into the Missouri mere weeks after the Bernard murder-suicide. It was an unusual coincidence in that winter of loss for both the college and the nation.

Arms folded, he continued to walk around the anteroom, taking it all in, when his thoughts were interrupted by the voice of a young girl.

Kara was all talk and smiles until she came out of the private door with her mother.

Pilate sank to one knee. "Hi, Kara. I'm John."

"This is Mr. Pilate," Kate said, correcting him.

"The man with the ticket!" Kara said. "Do you have an airplane?"

Pilate smiled. "No, I'm afraid not. They just call me that. I teach school with your mother at the college."

Kara seemed disappointed. She wanted to fly.

A lanky man with salt-and-pepper hair wearing a cardigan, corduroy pants, and a tie appeared in the doorway behind Kate and Kara. He slid an expensive fountain pen into his shirt pocket and smiled at Pilate.

Pilate rose to his feet.

"Hi. Grif Nathaniel," the man said.

Pilate recoiled mentally at meeting a storied bit player from the Bernard murders in the flesh. Nevertheless, he instinctively extended his hand. "John Pilate," he said, as the man shook it. "I teach at Cross."

"So Kate told me," he said. "Nice to see her taking a little time for fun." Nathaniel had a kindly manner that was betrayed slightly by the apparent sadness lurking behind his eyes.

Perhaps that's why they call him "Grief," Pilate thought.

"Grif, we are merely *co-workers*," she emphasized, cutting her eyes to Kara. "We were *at a meeting*."

Grif smirked. "Well, I hope it was a fun one nonetheless."

"We have to go. Say bye-bye to Grandpa." The mother dutifully nudged her daughter toward Grif for an embrace.

"See ya, sweet girl," Grif said.

"Bye, Grandpa," she said, pulling the hood of her coat over her head.

"Goodnight, sir. Nice to meet you," Pilate said with another look into the mortician's sad eyes.

Grif nodded. "Likewise." He hugged Kate for a moment. "Bye," he offered as the trio headed back out into the cold.

Pilate started the car and blasted the heater as high as it would go.

Grif waved from the door, and Kara waved back, as did Kate, albeit in a cursory way. "Nice man," Pilate said. Kate nodded.

"We were in Grandpa's lab!" Kara said with glee.

"I know, honey," Kate said. "Grandpa had some stuff he needed from downstairs," she said to Pilate, clearly irritated that Grif had taken the child into the embalming area.

"I see," he said, stopping for a moment as a long black Cadillac hearse eased past them and nosed into a covered portico on the side of the mortuary.

"Looks like we got here just in time," Kate said. "A new intake from the nursing home. Grif said it's Grace Hamilton. She was Dean Kennedy's secretary back when that crazy professor shot him."

Pilate glanced at Kara in the rearview mirror. "I see. Interesting."

They drove quietly; Kara had already dozed off in the back seat. "Thanks for doing this," Kate said. "We're just over this hill and down two blocks."

Pilate drove carefully, hyper alert to the black ice that tended to appear in sinister patches on overpasses.

"So, I noticed the picture of—" Kate cut him a look.

"Martin," Pilate finished, catching her drift.

"Oh," she said. "I never knew him. He died way back in the sixties."

"Grif's father?" Pilate said, already knowing the answer.

"Yes. From what Rick told me, he was a real town father-member of Rotary-chamber of commerce type. A good guy," she said. "Did he start the mortuary?"

"What are you, a cop?" she said, smiling through her put-on exasperation.

"Sorry. Just making conversation," he said.

"Next street."

"Okay."

"Well, to answer your interrogation, Officer, Martin's grandfather started it a long time ago—right around the time families stopped caring for their own dead, after the Civil War. You know, when it became uncivilized to have Grandma's corpse propped up in your front room for the days before burial."

"He died kind of young, didn't he?" Pilate said.

"A lot of men seem to in that family," she said.

Realizing what a damn fool insensitive thing he'd just said to Rick Nathaniel's widow, Pilate blurted "Oh, Kate, I'm sorry. I wasn't thinking. I am so sorry."

She looked out the window, pointing to a nice brick house with a large front yard. "This is it."

Pilate felt like a first-class ass. His ears reddened in embarrassment.

Kate pulled the sleeping Kara from the back seat. "It's okay, John," she said. Hoisting Kara to her chest, she looked Pilate in the eye. "And I'm okay too."

"Thanks for going to dinner," he said sheepishly.

"Sure. See you at school," she closed the car door and carried Kara up to the house.

"Stupid," John said aloud, punching the steering wheel.

Ollie Olafson was a large, powerfully built man with a thick Cro-Magnon brow that made sunglasses unnecessary even on the brightest of days. He guided his bulky frame into his late-model sport utility vehicle. He flicked on the radio, jammed a stubby cigar in his mouth, and steered the gas hog off the town's main street into a dark alley.

The longtime mayor of Cross Township, a job practically handed down to him from his late father, turned over the day's events in his mind: meetings with the developer and several phone calls from one town elder who demanded to know, "What are you gonna do about that asshole Lindstrom?" Ollie had assured them both that all the plans would go through just fine, as long as there were no "hiccups" at the last minute to queer the deal. He promised he would personally see to it that any case of the hiccups would be promptly cured. *That's why I'm out driving the fucking back roads at eleven o'clock on a ball-chilling night like this.*

After three blocks, he ran out of alley and onto a tree-lined gravel road that led to the hilltop location of Monticello Hill cemetery. The ancient cemetery commanded a view of Cross Township proper and Cross College during the day; this time of night, though, all he saw were the flicker of lights in homes and the firmament of twinkling stars overhead.

He pulled past the monuments of the cemetery. Some were standard obelisks; more than a few were poured cement in the form of trees with intricate vines, bark, and epitaphs. Beyond them lay the simple marble markers of the World War I and II dead, the ones killed in action and those veterans who'd been lucky enough to come home and live out their natural lives on American soil. His father's grave lay among them.

A few stray spires marked the resting places of a wealthy scion or favorite son of Cross, breaking up the monotony of stones until the rows stopped at a line of trees and a partially obscured path. Olafson stopped his SUV there; the vehicle was too wide to go any further.

The glow of his cigar preceded him as he trekked into a glen bathed in moonlight. He tripped twice on flat markers that had fallen over from long-dead border war and Civil War soldiers. They had nearly been forgotten until the cemetery board decided to make the area a protected place as they made application to the National Registry for the entire cemetery. Over his shoulder he saw the grim outlines of the Nathaniel family crypts, which had stood there since just after the Civil War.

"Dad?" Ollie heard his son's voice from the trees. "That you?"

"Yeah. Come on out," he said, exhaling Cohiba smoke.

Craig came out from behind a gargantuan oak large enough to conceal his bulk, his exhaled breath visible in the night air. "Hey, Dad."

"Hey. You make the call?" he said.

"Yup. Steve called in the accident. It should keep the sheriff tied up for a while, just in case."

"Well, you make damn sure that Steve keeps his fuckin' mouth shut. Tell him to stay off that hillbilly heroin so he doesn't go blabbin' off. You ready?"

The younger Olafson held a crow bar aloft in reply, the cold steel outlined in the moonlight.

"Let's do it," Ollie said. "Come on."

The hulking pair walked carefully through the garden of stone until they reached the crypts. Using a penlight, Ollie searched the names on the doors of each of the five crypts. The flashlight quit a couple of times, and Ollie shook it. "Piece of shit," he muttered. He struck it a couple times against his hand until the light returned. Ollie shined the light on the front of the crypt. "Nope," he said each time after looking at the names of the dead adorning the first three. "Yep," he said on the fourth.

Ollie stepped back. Craig lurched forward into the halo of the penlight and jammed the crowbar into the crypt door.

The wood was rotted at the hinges and gave way with a sickening crunch.

"Don't know my own strength," the younger man said with a snort.

"You never did," his father said, brushing past him into the darkness of the crypt. "Let's hurry, Craig."

The son shuddered, following his father into the house of the dead.

Pilate drove back to his apartment, trying to shake his feeling of stupidity. His selfish curiosity about a long-ago murder had hurt the feelings of a beautiful woman he really liked. Bringing up the untimely death of her husband was not an aphrodisiac.

Keyed up and unwilling to settle into his boring digs, Pilate steered away from the college, past his apartment toward downtown. Passing the scene of his bruised pride and jaw, heeding the warning from Krall about "another strike against him," Pilate rolled his eyes and kept driving.

Spurred on by his visit to the mortuary and too energized to sleep, Pilate decided a trip to the hilltop cemetery might be a good chance to have a much-needed smoke, and he was sure it would offer an even better view of the stars than his breezeway.

He turned on the car radio and began singing along to "Standing Outside a Broken Phone Booth with Money in My Hands." As he crooned along with the lyrics, he replayed the night's conversations with Kate to the point of his stupid remark, then cursed himself.

Driving slowly, he followed the green signs that pointed to the gravel road leading up to Monticello Hill. Not used to the unlit steep gravel road, Pilate felt even more stupid with every shimmy of his car on the gravel.

As he rounded a bend, the cemetery gates came into view about a quarter-mile away. Relieved, he sped up. Soon he could stop, look up at the stars, and get his nicotine fix.

A quick glance in his rearview mirror produced Simon's porcelain face. Sitting in the back seat, quiet for once, with his black pupils focused on the road ahead. He had a strange look on his face.

Is that...fear?

"Oh, would you please just go to hell?" Pilate said to his back seat stalker.

Simon merely sat there, his eyes widening. Then, as if prompted by some unseen force, he said, *"Look out, John,"* sounding detached.

An engine roar startled Pilate. He looked back toward the road and saw the high beams of a truck or SUV barreling down the gravel road, coming straight at him. Pilate jerked the wheel to the right, knowing the gravel road was by no means wide enough for his car and the big truck. He fishtailed, the Grand Am's rear end narrowly missing the truck as it sped past him. Momentum took over as Pilate fought to keep his car on the road. "Sh-i-t!" he wailed, stretching the four-letter word into three distinct syllables.

He felt the knuckles of both hands pop as he gripped the wheel. As he overcorrected, the car slid off the gravel road and rolled down the embankment about 100 feet, mowing down helpless, leafless saplings, small trees, and brush.

"I've been downhearted, baby..." was the last refrain Pilate heard before he cracked into a defiant oak tree and sank into blackness.

CHAPTER NINE

Pilate sat in a dark room, devoid of windows and doors. His head hurt. Music played—some kind of trance track he associated with dancing and watching kids do ecstasy.

"I told you to watch out, John."

"Shit," Pilate said, slowly turning his head upward to face Simon.

"Well, I have good news and bad news." His lighter clicked, and the smell of his cigarettes seemed more potent. *"The good news is that you are still very much alive."*

"I remember a...being in a car wreck."

"Yes, John. Very good," he said in that fucking singsong aristocrat accent.

"What do you want?"

Simon pulled up a chair in front of Pilate's—a chair that had not existed the second before. He straddled it, sitting backward, resting his alabaster chin on the back. *"Only to keep you company until you regain consciousness."* Smoke crept from his nostrils.

"You're too kind," Pilate said. "I think I'll wake up now. Good seeing you." Pilate shut his eyes in the dark room for a three-count. When he opened his eyes, Simon was gone, but Pilate was still in the room. His head hurt worse. "You think you're so smart, don't you?" Pilate said aloud to the empty room.

There was no answer.

Pilate closed his lids again. "I said, you think you're so smart, don't you?" Through his eyelids he saw a bright light.

"Well, I'm sure as shit smarter than you," Sheriff Scovill said, leaning over Pilate, shining a penlight in his eyes as he lay in the back of the sheriff's truck.

Pilate blinked twice.

"And I damn well know I'm a better driver."

"Oh…hi," Pilate said. "We really have to stop meeting like this."

Scovill clicked his tongue. "Uh-huh."

Pilate sat up. "Some guy blew me into the ditch."

"What? You got blown by some guy in the ditch?" Scovill teased, sniffing Pilate's breath.

"Does that qualify as a joke, sheriff?" Pilate was in no mood. His head ached, his car was in a ravine, and the asshole who'd knocked him off the road hadn't even bothered to help him.

"Close as I'm gonna get tonight." Scovill spat out a toothpick. "Mr. Pilate, from the tracks in the gravel, it looks like you tried like the devil to stay on the road. If you will indulge me in a breathalyzer, we can take your report."

Pilate aced the breathalyzer and shivered with cold.

"Get in," Scovill demanded more than offered.

"What about my car?" Pilate looked at its silhouette in the ravine. "It's screwed," Scovill said. "Now get in."

Pilate couldn't argue. At least it was warm in the sheriff's truck, and this time he got to sit in the front seat. He hoped there would be no farting.

The sheriff produced a weathered ticket book and notepad from a torn vinyl seat pocket. He looked at his watch and then called in to the station. "Lenny, this is Scovill. Come back," he said into the mic.

The static-ridden voice of his deputy replied. "Got ya loud and clear, Sheriff. Go ahead."

"Lenny, I have Mr. John Pilate. We got an 11-8-2 up by Monticello Cemetery. Has a nice knock on the head, but I think he's okay."

"He drunk?" Deputy Lenny said.

"Nope. He passed. I'll be back in shortly," he said.

"Out."

"Sorry to disappoint you." Pilate wanted a smoke, but he thought better of asking.

"Not disappointed, Mr. Pilate." Scovill started filling out the incident report. "But do you mind telling me what you were doing out here this late?"

"Just trying to clear my head," he said.

"Mm-hmm. And where were you previous to this?" Scovill scribbled on the report in the dim light of the truck's dome.

"Dinner in Goss City, with a colleague," Pilate said as blandly as possible. "You have an aspirin, by chance?"

"No. Which colleague?"

"I don't see what this has to do with anything, but I was with Kate."

Scovill looked up from his notebook. "Nathaniel?"

"Yes," Pilate said, looking him in the non-squinting eye.

"Shit. No wonder you need an aspirin," he said, a smirk growing across his rugged face.

"Can we get to the incident?" Pilate's head pounded.

"Incident or accident?"

The words hung in the air a second before Scovill said, "Okay, sure."

Pilate related the time and details of the incident to Scovill, who quietly transcribed the information in block-lettered handwriting to the report form.

"What kind of vehicle made you swerve?"

"Not sure. It was big though—either a large truck or SUV. It's so damn dark on these freaking roads."

"That's why most people with sense tend to avoid this road after dark, Mr. Pilate."

Pilate noted Scovill's frequent spasms of certain country wisdom paired with an attitude of what he could only call common-man supremacy. It was really irritating.

"So you can't tell me what vehicle, but you know the driver was a guy?"

"Well," Pilate said, "I mean, I can't be sure. All I really saw was a large shape for a split second. I was much more worried about watching the road than I was about the jackass who knocked me off it. If I find that asshole, I am going to rip him a new one."

"Easy, killer." Scovill scribbled some more notes.

"Sheriff, as you can see, I wasn't drinking. I was doing nothing wrong," Pilate said.

"Just minding your own business, huh?" He snorted. "Well, technically, you owe Charlie Forster for damages to his barbed wire fence, which you smashed through halfway down the ravine," he said, pointing with his ballpoint pen.

"Great."

"Hey, be glad that fence was there. It slowed you down before you hit the tree. You coulda been killed. Looks like you were going about forty-five. The crash woke Charlie and Marie up—well, the crash and your thick skull hitting your horn."

As if on cue, a scraggly-bearded older man appeared in the headlights, wearing a hunting jacket and cap that he'd hastily thrown on over pajamas. He ambled over to the sheriff's window and tapped on the glass with a boney knuckle.

Scovill rolled down his window. "Hey, Charlie."

"He okay?" the old man said, quaintly tipping his hat to them both.

"Yeah, just hit his head," Scovill said.

Pilate leaned toward the sheriff and Charlie and said, "Thanks for calling for help. I'm sorry about your fence. I'll pay for the damages."

Charlie's expression of weariness hardened. "Damn right you will, mister!" An awkward silence held for a moment until Charlie's face morphed into mirth. "Naw, forget about it. I'm just glad you're okay." Then he clapped Scovill's shoulder.

"Thanks. I'll get the car out of there tomorrow," Pilate said.

"Yup. Goodnight." Charlie walked back down the road toward a beaten-up mailbox by his driveway and disappeared into the darkness.

"Charlie's a good ol' boy," Scovill said. "Wouldn't pay seventy-five cents to see Jesus Christ in person, but he's still a good fella. You gave him a little excitement."

"My pleasure." Pilate rubbed his head. "So, any idea what you're going to do about this?"

He threw his truck into gear. "Not a hell of a lot, considering you can't identify the vehicle or the driver."

"Great," Pilate said.

"We'll ask around. Meantime, call Jimmy's Towing tomorrow to get your car out," Scovill said. "And you better hope Jack Lindstrom doesn't hear about this. I hate to say it, but you really aren't making a very good impression on your boss, Mr. Pilate."

"It just gets better and better," Pilate said.

Scovill dropped Pilate at his apartment with a squinty-eyed admonition to stay off the roads after dark.

Pilate took three Tylenol and collapsed, fully clothed, into bed.

In spite of his awful night, he managed to teach his classes the next morning. No one said a word to him about the accident. Kate wasn't in the office; she only had an afternoon class.

Drinking coffee and chewing aspirin he'd bummed off a student between his eight-thirty and ten-thirty classes, Pilate called Jimmy's to arrange for his car to be pulled from the ravine.

Jimmy audibly spat out a wad of tobacco and said he was available right away. He also offered to give the car a onceover after it was out of the ditch. He promised to pick Pilate up at noon on the road beside the oval.

Hanging up, Pilate rubbed his forehead a moment. He jumped when the phone rang a scant ten seconds later.

"Pilate? Trevathan," the dean barked. "Heard you cracked up your car last night. Come talk to me this afternoon."

Pilate explained he had to go fetch the car at noon.

"Then get over here soon as you're done," the line clicked. "Goddamn it," Pilate muttered, patting his pockets for a cigarette.

He stood on the edge of the ravine as Jimmy attached a towline to the rear bumper of his car and gently pulled it out.

"It don't look too bad," he said, giving the engine and frame a onceover, as he'd promised. "I'll take it back to the shop just to be sure."

"Thanks, Jimmy," Pilate said, scanning the gravel road for signs of the truck that had derailed him.

"Hey, there's the sheriff," Jimmy said, gesturing toward Scovill's now familiar truck that was heading toward them. From that angle, it looked a lot like the truck that had run Pilate off the road.

Scovill stopped in front of Jimmy's truck and climbed out of his own. He zipped up his coat, leaving the butt of his Glock peeking out a slit in the side, then walked over to the pair. "Bad?" he asked.

Pilate shrugged. "Anything new on the case?"

Scovill regarded him with his squinty eye. "You could say that."

"Oh?" Pilate said.

Scovill cut his eyes to Jimmy, who took the hint and went about the business of preparing to tow the car into town.

"When you were up at Monticello last night, did you see anything unusual?"

Pilate shuddered inside at the sudden change in temperature from the sheriff. "I never made it to the cemetery, Sheriff. Remember?"

The sheriff looked into Pilate's face as if his eyes were some kind of lie detector. "Oh yeah. I forgot." Scovill's demeanor relaxed. He looked over his shoulder at Jimmy.

"Why? Is something wrong at the cemetery?" Pilate said.

"No," Scovill said, taking a cinnamon toothpick from his pocket, "not unless you count grave robbing." And with that, he slipped the cinnamon toothpick into his mouth and arched his eyebrow at Pilate.

Scovill pulled into the cemetery, inching past the main yard slowly until he parked next to his deputy's truck. It rested at the mouth of a path that was too small for most cars. He put the truck in park, pulled the keys out of the ignition, and looked at Pilate. "Well, come on," he said. "You can see what happened up here last night."

Pilate slid from the truck seat and walked with Scovill down the path. Standing a few hundred yards away next to a series of crypts was Lenny, his deputy.

Lenny was a paunchy, bearded man. Pilate had not spoken to him much, but he'd seen him in town here and there—usually at the grocery store, where Lenny went to pick up a suitcase of beer.

"Anything new?" Scovill asked Lenny.

The deputy shook his head, his beefy frame leaning against the largest of the crypts, his bulk obscuring the names of the dead inscribed on the outside.

Pilate observed that the old door of the crypt had been ripped almost completely from its hinges and crumpled inward.

"Crowbar?" Scovill asked.

Lenny pointed at the lock, where telltale signs of a crowbar or pry bar of some sort still existed.

"Uh-huh," Scovill said, peering closer. "You concur, Mr. Pilate?"

Pilate smiled mildly and nodded. "You think it was kids? Vandals, just messin' around?"

"Coulda been." Lenny handed Scovill a plastic Ziploc bag. Scovill held it up and peered inside it at a red and white Cross College Cougars spirit ribbon, the kind worn on letter jackets and sweatshirts at pep rallies and basketball games. He then handed the bag back to Lenny and pulled a heavy flashlight from a loop on his belt and switched it on. "Come on, Mr. Pilate. Let's see if there are any tales from this crypt."

"Um, isn't this a crime scene?" Pilate sputtered. "I mean, shouldn't I stay out of there?"

Scovill turned his head halfway. "Well, yes, Mr. Pilate, you would generally be correct, except when the duly-elected sheriff of the county invites you into the crime scene, I suppose it's okay."

"Well, uh…why? I mean, thanks for thinking of me, Sheriff, but I really don't know why you want me in there."

Lenny poked Pilate's shoulder, more than a gentle nudge.

Pilate held his hands up in a gesture of contrition and followed Scovill into the crypt.

"Watch your step," Scovill said.

Pilate followed Scovill down four steps into a room that looked to be about twenty feet long and about twelve feet wide. The air was stale and still and smelled of the wet, moldy burlap sacks his brother used to push him into one summer in their grandparents' root cellar.

Scovill shone his light around until he found a Coleman lantern hanging on a hook beside the door. He lit and hung the hissing lantern from a hook on a rusty chain that dangled down in the center of the room.

When Pilate's eyes adjusted, he whispered, "Welcome to Castle Dracula."

Scovill grunted.

Lining each side were three large ledges that held the coffins lengthwise, one coffin per ledge. Three of the coffins looked extremely old, as if they'd seen at least seventy or eighty years. The three others looked newer, though exactly how new was hard to determine since they'd been smashed open. Actually, one was moved, but not opened.

A crumbling body lay on its face, spilling out of the coffin where it had been dragged off the ledge onto the floor. The perpetrators had apparently hacked away at the lid until it opened. The dead man's final suit was split up the back; Pilate had read once that morticians often cut the clothing of the deceased to make the job of dressing the corpse easier. The corpse's skin looked like old parchment, hanging off the ribs and backbone in dusty, webby hunks.

"Jesus," Pilate said, startled. "What the fuck?"

"Easy," Scovill said. He pointed his flashlight at the coffin across from the damaged one.

That casket, too, was open, though it still rested on the ledge. The corpse appeared to be that of an old woman. Steel-gray hair clung to the skull, with a thin layer of skin stretched over it; the eye sockets had long ago sunken in. Her decomposition was less advanced than the man's.

"Oh God. It's an old lady," Pilate said, gagging.

"Yup." Scovill examined the other coffins, which appeared undisturbed beyond the dust being wiped from the nameplates affixed to the sides. "Looks like they were looking for someone in particular."

"What do you mean?" Pilate said, straining to read one of the nameplates.

"Well, they apparently wiped the layers of dust off of each coffin, looking for a specific one. See?" He shone his Maglite on the nameplates. "They didn't mess with Rick's." The sheriff bowed his head.

Pilate cleared his throat; his gag reflex was kicking in. "What for? Did they molest the corpses or something?"

Scovill looked at him as if he were an alien.

"Well, what I mean is, was it like a corpse desecration—a revenge kind of thing—do you think?"

"I have no idea, Mr. Pilate."

"Sheriff, you can call me John if you want," Pilate said.

Scovill lowered himself down on his haunches over the corpse of the man. "Lenny?"

Lenny leaned in.

"You call the county medical examiner?"

Lenny nodded.

"Grief?"

He nodded again.

A man of few words.

"Good man." Scovill reached toward the body. "Mr. Pilate give me a hand. I want to look under the body."

"Oh, hell no! I can't do that," Pilate said, taking a step back.

"Look, I need help here," he said patiently.

"Well, what about Lenny?" Pilate said, his voice almost comically lowered so Lenny would not hear. "I mean, all he's doing out there is fantasizing about rabbits and beans with ketchup."

Scovill stood fully erect, facing Pilate, his flashlight shining under his face. "Mr. Pilate, these people are Lenny's relations. I can't hardly ask him to help me with this, now can I?"

"Shit. Sorry. I suppose it makes sense why he's staying outside then."

"Yeah, out of respect. He don't want to see them this way."

"You'd think people would be smart enough not to mess with a deputy sheriff's family," Pilate said.

"Well, first off, they have a different last name. Second, they're probably only third cousins," Scovill said. "You can't swing a dead cat in this county without hitting someone related to Lenny anyway."

"Nice," Pilate said. "Quite the metaphor."

"Meta-what?"

"Nothing. Let's do it." Pilate sighed and bent down over the body with Scovill. He gingerly placed his hands on the sides of the corpse's shoulders, where a living person's biceps would be.

"Okay, gently now, damn it. Pull the body toward you, and I'll have a look underneath," Scovill said.

To his relief, the corpse didn't have much of an odor. It felt like the straw scarecrow his grandparents used to haul out every planting season. It was still substantial, but it was light and not too difficult to move. "Uh…" Pilate said, encouraging the sheriff to hurry up.

"I'm looking," Scovill said, his head to the floor, with his light shining around underneath the corpse.

"Anything?"

"Uh-uh. Looks like somebody went through the pockets though. The shirt is untucked." Scovill whistled.

"What?"

"Well, the shirt's been unbuttoned too—torn open, like somebody was searching the body," he said.

"For what?" Pilate asked, disgusted.

"No idea, but you can put him down now."

Pilate eased the body down, rubbing his hands furiously on his pants.

"Don't worry. I don't think you got any zombie cooties on you," Scovill said.

Both heard a voice from outside the crypt.

"Sounds like Grief's here," Scovill said, walking up the stairs. "He's not gonna take this well."

"Well, at least it's repeat business," Pilate said, trying to lighten the mood.

"Mr. Pilate, I'm sorry if this whole thing spooked you a little, but that remark was really uncalled for." Scovill's jaw clenched around every syllable.

Before Pilate could reply in apology, a tall, thin silhouette filled the doorway. "Mom? Dad? Oh no. Oh no!" he said, his voice quivering.

"Grif, I'm so sorry," Scovill said.

Before Pilate exited the crypt, he took in the sorry surreal sight of Grif Nathaniel weeping quietly, gingerly cradling his father's corpse in his arms.

Outside, Pilate looked at Lenny as he walked a few feet away from Pilate, revealing the name "NATHANIEL" carved in the side of the crypt. Pilate stepped a few feet in the opposite direction and lit a cigarette, inhaling and exhaling the smoke into the cold air. The sun averted its gaze behind gray clouds.

He spied a white marble stone a few feet away, crooked and cracked, the name worn away by the elements and the passing of time. He glanced at his watch. *Shit. I've still gotta go see Dean Trevathan.*

Scovill appeared in the crypt doorway, zipping up his jacket. He put a hand on Lenny's shoulder, said something in his ear, and then walked over to Pilate. His squinty eye gazed past Pilate toward the college, which looked like a toy town from a train set in the valley below. "Thanks for your help in there."

"Sure. I'm, uh…well, I'm sorry about what happened," Pilate said. "I hope you don't think that uh…"

Scovill cocked his head and looked at Pilate. "What? That you broke into your new girlfriend's family crypt? Not fucking likely."

Pilate knew it was not time to argue the semantics of whether Kate Nathaniel was his girlfriend; especially since he was on a credibility-losing streak and the notion supported his alibi. "Exactly," Pilate said, turning to look down the valley. "Wait a minute! Wait just a damn minute. Do you think the guy who knocked me off the road did this?"

Scovill looked amused in that irritating way of his. "Well done, Sherlock."

"Well, that helps. How many students have trucks?"

"Students?"

"Well, you found a spirit ribbon, didn't you?" Pilate said.

"I also found Jesus when I quit drinking a few years ago, and I'm pretty sure He was in a tomb, too, but that don't mean nothing," Scovill said. "Even if we didn't find anything in there, logic dictates that it had to be somebody from around here, one of the locals. If that's the case, they more than likely work at, go to, or support the college in one way or another."

Pilate couldn't fault his logic. It could have been a student, an employee, or a booster for that matter. *Crap.* "So where does that leave us?"

"Us? I didn't know there was an us, but it leaves you on your way back to the college, Mr. Pilate." He turned on his heel and walked back toward the path. "With the thanks of the county for your assistance in our inquiries, of course."

Just as Pilate started to follow Scovill, Grif exited the crypt, blowing his nose into a handkerchief. "Sheriff, I'll wait with Lenny for the M.E.," he said. "When he's done looking over the remains, I'm going to take Mom and Dad over to the home and fix them up before they're re-interred."

"You bet, Grif. Just wait until Doc Hutton is finished before you move them around, okay?" His tone was uncharacteristically gentle.

Grif nodded and looked up at Pilate.

Pilate nodded, his face somber.

"Mr. Pilate was on the road last night when a potential suspect ran his car into the ditch," Scovill said. "He was here giving me his report."

"Oh, I see. Hello, Mr. Pilate," Grif said, the weariness behind his eyes unbearable. "Good to see you again."

"Yes, but I'm sorry it had to be…well, under these circumstances," Pilate said.

"Me too. In my line of work, I'm used to seeing people in their darkest moments," he said. "Odd to have the shoe on the other foot."

"Yes, well, if there is anything I can do," Pilate said.

"Thank you," Grif said. "There is one favor I'd like to ask, if you don't mind."

"Name it," Pilate said.

"Would you break the news about this to Kate for me? I am going to be a little tied up today, and it would be better if she heard details from a friend instead of through the grapevine. News travels fast and gets exaggerated around here."

"Sure. I'll tell her when I get back to the office," Pilate said, shaking Grif's proffered hand.

Pilate again wiped his hand furiously on his pants as soon as he was out of sight further down the trail.

"Nah, I don't think so," Jimmy said.

"Ever notice that the hottest girls in school are with the most dog-ugly, stupidest guys?" Krall said, catching up to Pilate on the oval after the sheriff dropped him off.

"Um, no, I hadn't noticed that," Pilate said.

"Where you going so fast?" Krall said, his hands jammed into his coat pockets against the cold.

"Got a meeting with Trevathan," he said.

"A meeting with the dean? What's up?"

"What? You haven't heard about my accident yet?" Pilate said.

"Nope. An accident, you say? You okay?" Krall answered, stepping up his pace.

"Fine," Pilate said. "Some idiot ran me off the road last night."

"Jesus. On purpose?"

"I sure hope not," Pilate said, "but they knocked me in the ditch on the cemetery road and kept on going."

"Wow. Man, it was probably just some drunk kids," Krall said.

"Yeah, drunk and hopped up on grave robbing," Pilate said, grasping the door of the Arts building.

"Ha. Good one," Krall said. "Oh…here." He handed Pilate a small box. "I grabbed your wireless card and password for you. I was just headed over to your office to give it to you."

"Thanks." Pilate pocketed the box, not losing a step.

"Let me know if you have any problems getting it to work. Anyway, I gotta go meet with Lindy's new hot-shit marketing guy. He wants to use the library as a centerpiece for his big media plan or some such shit. Fancy big-city idiot… wears a damn tie every day. See ya later." Krall peeled off to the library.

Pilate bounded past the dean's office and took the stairs two at a time. When he saw that Kate's light was on in her office. He stopped, took a breath, and knocked.

She didn't look up from grading papers. "Office hours are one to three today. It's past three."

"Kate," Pilate said.

She looked up. "Hi, John." She ran a hand through her sandy hair and put her pen down.

"Hi. Uh, I need to talk to you," he said.

"Oh, don't worry about last night. It's fine." She smiled, drawing those little crow's feet Pilate so loved to the surface around her eyes. "I had a good time," she said.

"Me too," Pilate said, taking the chair beside her desk. "Actually, I need to tell you about something else—about what happened last night after I dropped you off." Pilate related his experience from last night and the afternoon. He made sure she knew immediately that her husband's casket was untouched.

Kate listened, incredulous. The sorrow he had seen in her face the first time they met returned, and he hated that he had to tell her the ugly tale. "You must be kidding. You think our kids would break into a crypt?" Her head jerked as if she were miming spitting on the floor. "I mean, I know kids do weird shit when they're out getting drunk or high, and I've even heard of kids breaking into a crypt, but ransacking the coffins? God, Grif must be beside himself."

"Yes. He wanted me to tell you," Pilate said. "I get the feeling he doesn't have it in him to talk about it just now."

Kate looked at her hands, her palms resting upon her lap. "Who would want to do such a thing?"

"Kate, I'm sure Scovill will find the culprits." Pilate rose. "Trevathan really wants to see me now. Are you okay?"

"Yes. You better get to the dean's office," she said.

"Okay. Call me if you need...anything," he said.

Halfway out the door, Kate called him. "John?"

He leaned in the door. "Yeah?"

"Why were you all alone on that road late last night anyway?"

"Just out driving to nowhere in particular, to clear my head I guess."

"Clear it of what? Did something fill your head last night at dinner?" she said, her blue eyes suddenly cobalt.

"Um..." He looked at the floor, then back at her. He pointed to his wristwatch, shrugged, and walked out.

As he typed, Trevathan's reading glasses, perched on the edge of his nose, reflected the glare from the computer screen.

Pilate knocked.

"Oh, John Pilate," he said. "Come in and shut the door." He typed a few more keys. "Sit down. Be quiet a minute while I finish replying to this e-mail from our fearless leader."

Pilate complied. His eyes being quite good, he could read parts of the e-mail from his seat. The words *"fire him, misconduct, bad P.R."* and *"little asshole"* were prominent. Pilate's stomach churned.

A moment later, Trevathan finished his furious pecking of the keyboard; after a flourished stab at the enter key he turned to face Pilate. "You are what my sainted mother would call accident prone, Mr. Pilate," Trevathan said, taking off his glasses and tossing them atop a pile of papers on the walnut desk.

"Yes, but I got great marks in penmanship," Pilate said.

"You don't play well with others either," he said. "John, the proper response is, 'I know I've gotten off on the wrong foot here. I assure you that the accident last night was not my fault, but I do recognize that I need to be more responsible about staying out of situations that may embarrass this college'," Trevathan said, making a steeple gesture with his hands under his chin.

"Dean, are you telling me I'm fired?"

He looked at Pilate with his good eye; the glassy one roamed a few centimeters to the left. Trevathan blinked rapidly for a second or two. "No, but I can assure you that the odds of your contract being re-upped are very slim at this point," he said.

"The president of this college is very public relations-vigilant, and you have managed to create or be a party to a least two incidents that have reflected negatively on this college."

"Have I performed my duties poorly? Have I missed one class? Have you received one complaint about me from students?" Pilate's voice rose in anger.

"No, no, and no," Trevathan said, "but that doesn't matter anyway if the boss thinks you're a liability to his grand plan."

"I can go to the union," Pilate said.

"Yes, but you have no real standing, no history here or anywhere else." Trevathan sighed. "Besides, Lindstrom keeps the union president's balls in a jar on his desk next to the vase with the faculty senate's dentures."

"So I'm screwed?" Pilate said.

"Not quite," Trevathan said. "We still have two months left in the semester. Keep a low profile, stay out of trouble, and you might get some summer classes and an offer for next fall. Look, for precisely the fact that you are a good, solid teacher—which are in short supply here because Lindstrom has scared most of them away—I can beg poverty and get him to forget about canning you, but that won't happen if you fuck up again."

"I didn't fuck up. That car ran me off the road." Pilate raised his voice. "That jerk in the bar hit me without provocation. You were there. You saw it."

He nodded. "Why the hell do you think I'm fighting for you?"

Pilate let out a choppy breath, and his eyes watered.

"John, just lay low," said Trevathan in the most soothing voice he could muster. "Stay out of trouble. Stay home nights. Grade your papers," Trevathan said. "Watch TV. Read a book. Hell, write a book for all I care. Just stay out of trouble." He coughed into his clenched fist.

"So I'm to be a prisoner in my own apartment?" Pilate said. "What's next? Is Lindstrom going to tell me who I can eat lunch with? Who I can talk to? Maybe I should check in before I jack off?"

"That won't be necessary," Trevathan said, expressionless.

Pilate seethed, looking out Trevathan's office window a moment, taking notice of the slowly fading sun. "I'm sorry." He rubbed his forehead with a shaking hand. "It's been a hard year."

"I know." Trevathan's tone was fatherly. "This too shall pass."

"Yeah."

"Who knows? Maybe you'll find a job at some diploma mill in the Caribbean. I can write you a letter. On the other hand, maybe you can just tend bar on a beach and enjoy the scenery. I know a nice place."

Pilate rolled his eyes.

"How's your car?"

"I think it's okay. Jimmy's giving it a onceover to be sure."

"Good. Why don't you go home?" Trevathan stood up.

"Nowhere else to go, is there?" Pilate managed a half-hearted smirk as he opened the door and strode into the hallway.

"Who likes conch fritters anyway?" Trevathan said.

PILATE'S CROSS

CHAPTER TEN

Pilate lay on his couch smoking, a vodka and Sprite nearly untouched on the coffee table. His answering machine had cheery news: He had cracked the radiator against the tree, and Jimmy would have his car for a few days. *I really am a prisoner.*

Looking at the ceiling, his thoughts turned back to the cemetery. *Why,* he mused, *would someone be searching long-dead bodies? And for what? Just the bodies of the undertaker and his wife were disturbed. Clearly they were the ones the grave robbers were searching for. But why?*

Pilate sat up, drank some of the vodka, and tapped his ashes into a black ceramic typewriter-shaped ashtray his grandfather had given him. The face of the frustrated novelist young Pilate idolized flashed through his mind. He pushed out the maudlin memory, focusing again on the cemetery, and he picked up his phone and dialed.

"Hey," Krall said, answering without saying hello.

"Hey," Pilate said.

"You asshole. Why didn't you tell me about that grave robbing thing today? Shit, I thought we were friends," Krall said.

"I was going to, but Trevathan wanted my ass in his office, so I had to hurry," Pilate said. The real reason was that he'd been so disturbed by the whole thing that he wasn't ready to talk about it.

"Besides, I figure if somebody farted in this town, you would have smelled it before I could tell you."

Krall laughed.

"Has this sort of thing happened before?" Pilate asked.

"Farts?" he said, then laughed at his own childish joke.

"Ha. Seriously, the grave thing," Pilate said.

"Oh, some kids got caught kicking over gravestones a few years back, just punk drunk crap like that," Krall said. "I think I heard that some Goth gang broke into one of the crypts once, too, but they just smoked pot, burned a few candles, and acted depressed about their mascara. They didn't disturb the coffins."

"Well, nobody smoked pot in there this time, I don't think," Pilate said.

"Lenny told Lonnie Porter down at the store that you were up there helping the sheriff," Krall said, his voice rising an octave. "Were you really in there?"

"Lenny can talk?" Pilate asked.

A beat.

"Yes, Krall. I was up there getting my car out of the ditch, and the sheriff picked me up and dragged me in there," Pilate said. "But let's keep that quiet on campus. I don't need the rumor mill going."

"Too late, man. I already knew you were there, and I know Lindstrom's ears have reported in to command central," Krall said.

"True." Pilate recalled his conversation with Trevathan.

"So what did you see?" Krall sounded like an anxious teenager digging for details on a buddy's first screw.

"What else did Lenny say?"

"Not much," Krall said. "As you know, he's a man of few words. From what I could glean, a couple coffins had been smashed in. I think he said Martin and Millie Nathaniel's? Anyway, they said it looked like someone was searching the coffins for something."

"That was what it looked like," Pilate said. "Were they buried with expensive jewelry or something?"

"Doubt it—especially not with a body in a crypt. That'd be so much more vulnerable to theft than a body in the ground. Poor Grif. This has to be hard for him, having to put his own folks back together." Krall actually sounded sincere.

"Yes," Pilate said, recalling Grif at the crypt earlier.

"How's Kate?"

"Fine. I told her." Pilate kept his tone neutral.

"Well, she and Kara are really all Grif has left, ya know?"

"Yeah."

"She may need someone to lean on," Krall said. The leer in his voice was impossible to miss.

"You're a dick, Krall," Pilate said.

"You know your own kind, I see," he said with a laugh. "Let's go down to the bar and get a drink. Birds of a feather oughtta drink together, don't ya think?"

"Can't. Presidential house arrest."

"Fucking Lindstrom," Krall said. "I can come by."

"I'm kind of tired anyway, Krall."

"Well, is your Internet card working?"

"I haven't used it yet, but that's not a bad idea. It'll help me kill time here in solitary."

"Glad I could help. Check out some porn and let me know if you hear anything new—or see any videos worth checking out."

"Will do."

After Pilate hung up, he gulped down his drink, lit another cigarette, and lay back on the couch. He surveyed the room, his eye landing on the worn copy of *Modern Criminal Investigation*.

Pilate grunted, fetching the wireless card from his coat pocket. He plugged it into his laptop and typed in the password Krall had scrawled on the box: "*poontang.*" He rolled his eyes, sighed and followed the instructions.

Once he was online, Pilate retrieved the e-mail from his personal account. A lot of spam had clogged his inbox. After spending about twenty minutes filtering out the junk mail, he focused on the e-mail from his friends and family.

His parents had written a short, sweet note of encouragement about his "new adventure," advising him to "keep his eye on the ball." Pilate was confident his father had written that one.

Pilate wrote back to his parents and a few other friends, then surfed some blogs and news sites for a while. Within an hour, he had tired of surfing and turned off the computer. He wasn't even slightly tempted to click through porn sites—at least not yet.

The next morning, Pilate rose early after a fitful night in bed. Around six thirty, he journeyed across the chilly oval to the cafeteria, frost crunching under his feet.

In the cafeteria, about twenty student zombies milled down the serving line, pointing and grunting at the sight of French toast, eggs, bacon, sausage, or Froot Loops.

Pilate ordered scrambled eggs, bacon, toast, and coffee for himself, then took a seat alone by a window overlooking the oval.

Halfway through his eggs, he spied Jack Lindstrom making his walk from the modest president's residence at the south end of the oval to his office in the admin building at the north end. He walked with a spring in his step. Thinning hairs on his head waved in the breeze.

Pilate indulged in a sneer as he crunched on his bacon.

"Is it that bad, Mr. Pilate?"

Pilate turned to see Abbey Prince standing beside his table, dressed in unflattering sweatpants, a Cougars sweatshirt, and a ball cap, with her brown hair sticking out the back in a ponytail. In spite of her very non-feminine attire, Abbey was pretty in a fresh-scrubbed, corn-fed, farm girl way—the absolute epitome of the girl next door. She was in his speech class on Mondays and Wednesdays.

"Huh?" he said.

"The bacon. You made a face," she said.

"Oh yeah." He wanted to tell her that he was actually making a face at the biggest asshole on campus, but he could only assume that would not be proper. "It's a little burnt. I prefer it chewy."

"Oh, me too. Absolutely!" she said.

Pilate thought his student unnaturally perky for this time of day.

She hovered, holding her tray and glancing at the table. "Abbey, would you care to join me?" he said.

She seemed to smile with her entire body. "Sure." Abbey sat with one chair between her and Pilate. Her ponytail flopped as she removed her hat and appeared to say a silent prayer over her food. Seconds later, she was spearing scrambled eggs using a fork with two bent tines.

"Was that a prayer?" Pilate asked.

"Yes," she said. "Sometimes I give thanks for my food, but mostly I pray I won't eat too much."

Pilate wasn't sure if she was serious and had no idea how to respond without insulting her.

Fortunately, she let him off the hook with a laugh. "You can take the girl out of the farm..." she said.

Pilate liked Abbey. She was studying to be a special education teacher and was one of the brighter lights among the students he taught.

"I think it's nice," he said, eating a corner off a piece of buttery wheat toast.

"Mama and Daddy made me promise I would," she said.

"So they're farmers?"

"Yes," she said, a little put out. "Remember my speech on my family history?"

"Right," Pilate said. "Sorry. I have more than a hundred students to keep track of."

"Sure," she said, drinking skim milk from a plastic tumbler.

"So, Abbey, how's everything?"

"Oh, okay," she said. "School's all right. Grades are pretty good. I start student teaching next semester."

"Well, you've worked very hard," he said. "As I recall, you're already a senior after two years. No breaks, huh?"

"Nope," she said. "I just wish I had taken a little more time to have fun, though, ya know?"

"Yes, I understand," Pilate said.

Abbey's features made the shift from slightly heavy teenager to curvy woman at that very moment.

"I rushed through my bachelor's degree too."

"Did you have any fun?" she said, looking over her milk at Pilate in a way that suggested something a far cry different than the ring toss at the county fair.

He smiled. "That is none of your business."

"Oh come on, Mr. Pilate! You can tell me."

"No, no I can't, Abbey." He ate more wheat toast.

"Does anyone ever call you Mr. Pill-ot-ees?" she asked.

"Never more than once," he said.

She finished her milk.

He surveyed her face a moment. She really was pretty. He indulged in a small fantasy as she finished her eggs. *If I were a lot less damaged and a few years younger,* he thought, *this young lady would be sharing my bed.*

"So you're not married, are you?" she said, startling him a little from his impure reverie.

"Um, no," he said.

Her eyes darted from his plate to hers. "Divorced?" she said, looking at her bacon. She said it as if the concept were worthy of shame but that she could make an exception in Pilate's case.

"Yes," Pilate said.

"What happened?"

"Life," Pilate said, putting the toast down and wiping his mouth with a paper napkin. He suddenly felt old, used up, and sickened at his thoughts of bedding the innocent girl.

"Oh I'm sorry, Mr. Pilate," she said, her eyes a little moist. "I just think you're such a neat guy. Whoever she was, she must have been crazy to leave you."

"How do you know *she* left *me*?" Pilate said, smiling as he stood up. "See you in class."

"Bye, Mr. Pilate. See ya," she said, her bright smile returning, though her cheeks were flush with embarrassment.

"Abbey?" he said, stopping and walking back to her. "Yes?" she said, turning to him.

"You're neat too," he said, smiling. Abbey smiled back, relieved.

Pilate put his tray in the return, walked to the door, and ran into Kate, who was just on her way in. "Hi," he said.

"Hi," she replied. "You okay?"

"Sure, but I was going to ask you the same question," he said. "It was a rough night, but we made it, thanks to Curious George, chocolate milk, and graham crackers."

"Okay. Well, if there's anything you need—" Pilate started to say.

Abbey appeared behind them and interrupted him. "Mr. Pilate, could I come by during office hours?" She glanced at Kate. "Oh, Miss Nathaniel, hi. Sorry to interrupt. I didn't see you."

Kate nodded, turned away three-quarters, and rolled her eyes.

"Um…sure, Abbey. Come on by," Pilate said.

"It's a date!" Abbey said, perky as ever. The door closed behind her as she bolted back to her dorm.

"You really shouldn't date your students," Kate said.

"Hilarious," Pilate said.

"You were saying, before your girlfriend interrupted?"

"I was just saying if you need anything…" Pilate said, his hands in his front pockets, looking at the floor like an embarrassed schoolboy.

"How about a drink Friday night?"

"That sounds good," Pilate said, "but you'll have to drive. My car's in intensive care at Jimmy's."

"I can handle that," Kate said. "But do me a favor in the meantime."

"Anything," Pilate said.

"When you have your date with Abbey, ask if she babysits," Kate said, gently poking Pilate in the arm as she walked away.

Like a good boy, Pilate went to work. He taught his classes, graded papers, and met with the other instructors for an in-service meeting about plagiarism. Kate attended with him and eight other instructors. They listened to Dean Trevathan talk about the hazards of online rip-offs of source material for term papers.

Pilate stole a glance at Kate, who sat on the opposite side and far end of the conference table. She was earnestly taking a few notes, carefully ignoring Pilate's attempts to catch her eye.

Afterward, Pilate retreated to his deserted office. Abbey strolled in just long enough to ask about the next class assignment and make a couple of thinly-veiled queries about Pilate's sex life.

"That Riley Pierson sure is a nice guy," Pilate said.

"He's immature," Abbey said with a pout. "He peed his pants on the bus in grade school." She crinkled her nose.

"People change. You wouldn't believe what I did in high school to this obnoxious guy in the school play," he said.

"What?" she asked, her face alit.

"Let's just say it involved a harmonica and something, uh…unhygienic. The point is, you shouldn't judge people by one event in their lives, right?"

She nodded.

He shooed the oversexed coed from his office and locked himself in.

Pilate didn't really have much to do, but he just couldn't face a return to his depressingly lonesome apartment. It was Thursday, and the next night promised more time with Kate. She would be a welcome diversion from the bizarre happenings of the past few days and his paranoid thoughts, but until then, he had to entertain himself somehow.

He straightened his desk, glancing at the photo of his parents. He thought about calling them, but decided he wasn't really in a talking mood. His mother would sense his anxiety and start to worry anyway; and Pilate's mother had enough problems of her own.

The office was like a prison cell in its dimensions and pretty warm from the unmanageable steam heating system employed by the nearly century-old building. Pilate opened the window that overlooked a small alley between the Arts building and admin. A gust of cold January air revived him in an instant.

He wanted a cigarette, but he knew that would be playing right into the hands of fate. With his recent luck, he'd set off some hidden smoke alarm, even with the window open. *I guess I used up all my good fortune at that Indian casino,* he thought.

Another gust of wind whistled through the window, blowing several graded papers off his desk and onto the floor next to his book bag. As he scooped them up, the 1963 murder file in his bag caught his eye.

Pilate replaced the papers on his desk and tucked the thick murder file envelope under his arm as he reached over to close the window.

Falling wearily into his chair, he opened the envelope and flipped through the photocopies until he found a story printed in the journal of the state historical society. Written about twenty years after the murders occurred, it turgidly put all the details together in a neat bow, citing "moral decay" as the culprit.

"Is this how you take your mind off grave robbers? Reading about an old murder?" Simon teased from over his shoulder.

Pilate ignored the voice.

"You haven't taken your pills in two months." This time, Simon's tone was a nagging I-told-you-so. *"Aren't you having trouble concentrating?"*

Pilate indeed was having trouble concentrating, and he'd been doing reckless things. Probably for the first time in years, he was completely off the antidepressants that usually kept him on an even keel. His moods went from elation to depression in a matter of hours. Fortunately he was good at concealing the churning seas inside him from people, as long as he didn't have to spend much time around them.

"That's why you didn't call good old Mom, huh? She'd know in two sentences how crazy you are right now," Simon said. *"And she knows from crazy."*

He hadn't been sleeping well, and intellectually, he knew he was beginning to feel more than slightly paranoid. The problem was, once he became paranoid, his intellect couldn't save him from its effects. The emotional side took over, as if he were a spectator watching himself perform an erratic show.

"Paranoia…or is it reality?" Pilate said aloud.

"You tell me," Simon said. *"That doctor cleared you years ago of being schizophrenic. You're just severely depressed. You don't actually hear my voice, do you?"*

Pilate felt an odd comfort to be reminded that he merely had bouts of severe depression—hellish, yes, but it was still preferable to schizophrenia. "Then why don't you go away?"

"Everyone needs a hobby," Simon said.

The question of who Simon was would have to take a back seat to the matters at hand. "Well, someone did run me off the road."

"Were you just in the way of someone in a hurry? A drunk driver, perhaps?"

"I have no idea," Pilate said, pinching the bridge of his nose. "I just know I can't stay here forever."

"The way you're going, I don't think that will be much of an issue." Simon chuckled. *"Besides, Sam called you again, didn't she? She obviously still cares."* He said the last three words like a giggly schoolgirl would if the star quarterback winked at her.

"She was drunk."

"Well, sometimes a strong drink brings out the strongest feelings, you know. Mr. Vodka lets the old guard down."

Pilate rubbed his forehead with his palm. "You're not real, Simon," Pilate said. "You really can fuck off now. Just get out of my head."

"I can only assume you want me in your head. Otherwise you would refill your prescription," he said.

"First thing tomorrow, I will, buddy. You can bank on it."

"Tough to get to the Goss City pharmacy/five-and-dime soda fountain without a car," Simon said. *"Besides, do you really want Opie and Andy and everyone in Mayberry knowing you take those embarrassing antidepressants?"*

"Why would I be embarrassed that I need medication? It's just that I don't need Lindstrom using it against me, and —"

Pilate's phone jingled.

Simon evaporated.

"Hello?"

It was Abbey, who claimed she'd "forgotten to mention" that she was going bowling that night in Goss City and that it would "totally rock" if he came along.

He made his apologies, telling her "some other time."

Her pout was nearly audible.

He hung up the phone, smiling. Yawning, he started to put the old historical society article about the murders back in the envelope when a word in the story caught his eye. *"Cremated. Professor Bernard's body was cremated, though his family never claimed his cremains."* Pilate reread the sentence twice, then the paragraph, and then the complete story. *Cremains? That's a new one.* As of the 1980s, no one from Bernard's family had claimed his ashes from the Nathaniel Mortuary. Pilate clicked a pen against his front teeth. *What happens to a person's ashes if nobody claims them?*

Back at his apartment, he powered up his computer and used Krall's password to access the library's LexisNexis account and the Internet. Once he got into the college network, he did a Web search on cremated remains, *cremains* being his keyword.

He wasted an hour surfing between horror stories of mistreated human remains. For starters, the director of a Georgia funeral home had claimed to be cremating people but was instead stacking the rotting corpses in a storage shed. He'd substituted concrete dust and wood chips for ashes.

His need for news of the prurient satisfied, he surfed until he found what he was really searching for. Many mortuaries are faced with the problem of families not understanding that cremation in itself is not the final disposition of remains. Several articles revealed stories of ashes stored in mortuaries for years, even decades.

One funeral director had the ashes of more than 200 people in his care. The director was quoted as saying he had tried all avenues to contact next of kin, to no avail. So, he reported he was going to bury the ashes in his cemetery and be done with them. "These are human remains, after all," he said. "You wouldn't leave an intact body lying around for decades, would you?"

Pilate wondered if Brady Bernard was still "lying around" Nathaniel's Mortuary. Krall had mentioned a tornado that had hit in the 1980s, followed by a fire a few years later. An Internet search of the *Cross Courier's* archives verified his reports.

The cremains of Brady Bernard could have been inadvertently discarded then or unceremoniously buried since…or put in a vault.

His eyes throbbing, Pilate shut off the computer and crawled into bed. He could only think about Friday, about tomorrow, about Kate.

Drinking coffee in the small café overlooking the student union fitness center, Pilate eyed Abbey Prince through the condensation-fogged glass as she exercised. She wore her hair in pigtails. She stretched, putting her farm girl posterior pleasantly in view.

"Sure, she's pretty," Krall said, "but two years after you marry that gal, her ass will spread out like a week's washing."

Pilate waved him off.

"But man, what a ride in the meantime, huh?" Krall leered over his coffee cup.

"You're a dirty old man, Krall," Pilate said. He looked down at the packets of sugar he was aimlessly arranging on the table in front of him.

"A badge of honor I wear proudly on my shabby breast," he said. Friday was crawling by; Pilate's only class of the day was done. He'd been meeting Krall for coffee and a chat in the student union the past few Fridays.

"Krall," Pilate said, "something's really been bugging me."

"What?" Krall looked over his shoulder at a gaggle of girls coming in from the cold and rushing up to the counter.

"The whole crypt thing," he said.

"Yeah, I've been meaning to ask you about that. Why the hell did Scovill invite you along to that little picnic?"

"Not sure." Pilate shrugged. "I thought it was odd, too, but maybe he thought of me as a disinterested party who could offer an objective opinion. His deputy was upset. Or he may have thought I did it and was hoping I'd trip myself up. Don't know. I just wish I could say I hadn't seen that stuff."

"Well, have ya heard anything new?" Krall said.

"No. You?"

Krall shook his head. "Not a peep. I think the whole thing's got Scovill flummoxed."

Pilate swallowed a sugary mouthful of coffee. "Why would anybody want to break into Martin and Millie Nathaniel's coffins?"

Krall's face took on a pained look, as if he were working out a tough math problem. "You got me. Probably just a stupid, meaningless prank."

Pilate gestured at the girls and at a couple of young men who were studying at a table. "Do any of these kids look like ghouls to you? Heck, eighty percent of the kids who come here came from a twenty-five mile radius," Pilate said. "Surely they'd have no interest in digging up the dead, especially since half of them are related somehow. And the other kids, the ones from the city, would be scared to death of pissing off the locals. I just don't buy the student prank explanation."

"So you read the new marketing guy's demographic report, eh? You've really put some thought into this, haven't you?" Krall said.

"Well, when you're nearly killed by a truck speeding away from the scene of the crime and then the local constabulary introduces you, up close and personal, to Grif Nathaniel's decomposing ancestors..."

Krall watched Abbey as she chugged away on the Stairmaster. "Work those glutes, Abigail," he said shamelessly.

Pilate tossed a sugar packet on the table.

Krall manage to jerk his lustful gaze from Abbey's hips to face him again. "John, can I give you some advice?"

Pilate smirked; up to that point, Krall had never called him John. "Sure, Derek."

"Leave it alone." Krall looked back at Abbey.

"What do you mean?"

"John, there's obviously something weird going on, but it's not your concern." Krall seemed to be making an effort to keep his tone light, though he would not—or could not—meet Pilate's gaze anymore. "You're here for a few more months at best, right? I mean even if Lindstrom doesn't run you off, it's apparent that you don't fit in at Cross. That's been clear right from the start, truth be told...and I mean that in the kindest way possible."

Pilate nodded slowly. "Okay, fair enough. I don't disagree.

But I have to know....uh, do you have a theory?"

"Yes, yes I do," Krall said, "but I am not going to go into it."

"Why?"

"Because I think you would start nosing around in it and get your ass shot by somebody," Krall said in a whisper.

"What the hell do you mean?"

"John, you should be smart enough to figure out that there're people in this town who run things, and they don't like outsiders messing around."

"Jesus, Krall. This sounds like an episode of the *Incredible Hulk* or something." Pilate laughed. "Every time Bill Bixby wandered into town he'd start messing around with somebody's perfect scheme or the mayor's daughter would get all gooey over him and then all hell would break loose."

"Well, unless you can turn into a super-strong green mutant, I suggest you end this episode now," Krall said.

"Actually, when I get angry, I do change. It's a bitch because I always ruin a pair of purple pants," Pilate said. "You know how tough it is to find those?"

Krall smacked the table with his open hand.

Several students looked up for a moment, and then turned back to their books and conversations.

"John, listen to me. This is not a joke. People have been murdered in this town before, and I wouldn't put it past happening again."

"I know. The Bernard thing, remember?"

"Among others," Krall looked around conspiratorially. "John, people who don't mind their own business around here often find themselves in the river or with a bullet in their head —or both. Those are the kinds of people who research things instead of leaving well enough alone."

"Krall, I can tell you're serious, and I appreciate your concern." Pilate sat up in his chair. "Look, I just want to finish up here and move on. I have no interest in getting killed. Just give me an idea for my own curiosity. Shit, I deserve at least that."

Krall sighed deeply. "All right, but keep your mouth shut about it, especially to Kate."

Pilate nodded hurriedly.

Krall laid his long boney-fingered hands on the table in front of him. "There are people in this town who stand to make a lot of money on some upcoming land deals."

Pilate felt a little disappointed. *Land deals? Not exactly the stuff of great mysteries.* "Um, okay."

"Let me finish. Legend says that back in the day when Bernard offed the president and dean here, it might've had something to do with a bad business deal that involved Ollie Olafson's dad, who was mayor back then. He was also head of the local Klan Klaven."

"Nice," Pilate said.

"There's a rumor that Martin Nathaniel was in on it, but he got cold feet and threatened to spill the beans to save his own ass. That was why he was killed."

"Killed? I thought he had a car accident."

"Sure. Somebody *accidentally* ran him off the road," Krall said.

"Holy crap."

"Yeah, exactly. Crap is putting it lightly, and there wasn't anything holy about it. See why I'm worried, now, Speed Racer?"

"Yeah." Pilate rubbed his temple. "But why go rooting through the coffins?"

"There is also a longstanding rumor that Marty had some evidence—something that would burn the Olafsons to the ground. Until now, I just assumed it was either a false rumor or that Olafson had found the evidence or whatever, but now I gotta wonder if there's more to it than that."

"If something was in those coffins, that would mean that somebody had to have put it there," Pilate said.

"Well, any one of a hundred people coulda slipped something into Marty's coffin."

"But Millie died years later, right? Why search hers?"

"I don't know for sure. Maybe to make it look less suspicious?" Krall shrugged. "Or maybe somebody thought something was hidden in there."

Pilate's thoughts rattled around in his skull for a few seconds. "Grif! What about Grif? Would he know something?"

"Well, it's been a long, long time, and nobody's bothered Grif that I know of," Krall said, holding his coffee cup aloft for a refill from the student passing by with the pot. "Of course, there wasn't anybody trying to buy land to put in a golf course and shopping center on the edge of town until now."

Pilate was silent as the student warmed up his coffee too. "So you think Olafson is ransacking graves trying to find something that could incriminate his family and queer the real estate deal?"

"That's my theory, John." Krall sipped his hot coffee. "Then again, I could be crazy."

"Interesting." Pilate's mind jumped from fact to fact.

"John, that faraway look in your eye better stop now. You promised to stay out of this. They're not playing around." Krall leaned forward. "I mean it, man. Just do your job, have some fun...screw some students." He nodded toward Abbey as she did crunches. When he saw the scowl on John's face, he continued, "Or don't. Date Kate Nate. Do whatever you want to do, then move on after summer semester. Take this advice, John. It might just save your life."

"Okay, Krall. Thanks for sharing," Pilate sipped his coffee a moment. "I'll behave.

"Well," Krall continued, once again envying the workout gear that had the chance to hug Abbey's notable rear end, "nobody said you had to behave *too* much."

CHAPTER ELEVEN

Kate knocked at his door around six.

"Welcome to Pilate's Place," he said, tucking in his shirt and gesturing to the small living room.

Kate looked around; she had a wry smile on her face. "Bachelor heaven, I see."

"That bad?"

"Actually, no," she said, sounding a bit surprised. She slid her purse and coat off and laid them on a chair. "More books than most bachelors, and…" She wandered around the room. "So far, the place seems almost completely devoid of jock stuff."

"Does fencing count? I was a champion swordsman in college," Pilate said.

"More aesthete than athlete, huh?"

"Good one. And yes. Won't you sit down?"

Kate sat on his well-worn couch.

"Would you like a glass of wine before we go?" Pilate took a couple steps toward the kitchen, anticipating her answer.

"Sure. Do you have any Cab?"

"I do." Pilate had the nicest six-dollar Australian Cabernet in his wine rack. He removed the cork, poured two glasses, served Kate, and then sat beside her.

She sipped her wine and nodded approvingly. "Nice."
"Thanks. It's from an insouciant little vineyard run by Crocodile Dundee."

She chuckled and swallowed some more. "How was your day?"

"Oh, okay," he said, looking into his glass. "Yours?"

"Good. Got caught up on some paperwork at least."

"You get a babysitter for Kara?"

She sighed heavily. "No. Actually I struck out. Most of the college girls I use went home for the weekend, and the high school girls I usually call are in a school play tonight."

"Let me guess...*Our Town?* Wait...did you leave Kara on her own?"

"Yes, John, but don't worry. She's perfectly safe. I left a loaded pistol for protection and a bottle of Jack Daniel's, just in case she gets thirsty." She sipped more wine.

"Grif has her?"

"Uh-huh. Boy, John, you're sharp for a city boy." She smirked.

"Well, we could have canceled. I know Grif has his hands full right now," Pilate said, drinking more of his own wine.

"He does, but I think a little time with Kara will help him take his mind off things. If nothing else, she'll keep him out of the mortuary," Kate said, "and frankly, I needed a break myself."

She looked into Pilate's eyes in a very deliberate way.

His skin tingled; he hadn't felt that in a long time. A few weeks without antidepressants, along with the lure of pirated porn, had revived his libido quite nicely. Kate was the final bit of encouragement he needed. Pilate took her glass and set it beside his on the coffee table. He kissed her lightly on the mouth.

Her lips were firm for a perceptible second, then melted around his. Her tongue gently swam into his mouth as he cupped her cheek in his hand.

They kissed for a few moments, then broke apart a few inches—just enough to look into each other's eyes. Hers sparkled, dewy and half-lidded. Pilate's hand moved from her cheek to her neck. He felt the warm flush on her skin, her pulse increasing.

She let out a low moan as he touched her breast through her shirt and kissed her neck. Her hands pressed against his chest.

Pilate laid Kate back on the couch and moved on top of her. Her body rose to meet his as his hand felt her ass. He was not disappointed in the firm, muscular butt that moved with his kisses and the exploration of his hands.

She squealed with delight as he playfully nibbled her lower lip. She pressed her lap against his. The volume of her moans increased when he opened the buttons of her jeans and slid his hand under her panties.

He felt her lush, soft pubic hair and explored her mouth deeply with his tongue as he slid his fingers inside her. Kate felt silky and warm to his touch.

She grasped the sides of his head and put her lips to his ear. "I want you inside me, John."

He kissed her, reared up, and pulled her Levi's and underwear off. Before she could protest, Pilate was kissing her and using his tongue instead of his fingers.

Kate rocked back and forth, her hands running through his hair, pulling it gently as he flicked his tongue inside her. Pilate's own excitement grew, and by the time Kate climaxed from the labors of his tongue, he was ready to go further.

As Kate lay back, breathing heavily, smiling with pleasure, Pilate stripped off his clothes, then removed her shirt and bra.

He looked at her firm body for a moment, long enough for her to become self-conscious and place her hands over the scar left over from her caesarian section.

"Hey," he said softly, gently moving her hands and kissing the scar.

She looked at him with trusting eyes as his body merged with hers.

Moonlight streamed through the blinds as they lay there.

Pilate really, really wanted a cigarette. He was disgusted with himself for slipping so far back into his pathetic addiction, but at that moment he desperately needed a smoke.

Kate's hands rested on his, clasped on her belly as he held her, her back to his chest, her head resting in the crook of his arm.

"Isn't this where we have a smoke?" Kate said.

"Um, are you serious?" Pilate said.

"Yeah. I mean, you do smoke, right? I do after orgasms. So…" she said.

"I didn't know you knew I'm a smoker."

"John, as nice as your apartment and hygiene is, I can smell it on you," she said.

"Oh. Do you really want one?"

"Yes, but don't take this as a sign that I approve of it," she said. "I mean, I only have one after good sex."

"Uh-oh," Pilate said, standing up to fetch his cigarettes from his coat pocket.

"What?" she said, covering up with a throw.

"Well, in that case, I hope this doesn't lead to you being a pack-a-day girl. Or then again, maybe I do," he said with a wink.

"Lame, Pilate," she said, reaching for her wine. "Just lame." Pilate lit two cigarettes, a la Clark Gable, and handed one to Kate. She puffed it like a pro.

"It was really wonderful," he said.

"Yes, but can we not talk about it? Can we just let it be what it is?"

Pilate nodded. "Sure."

"Besides," she said, sitting up, "I'm hungry."

They sat on the living room floor, scarfing down grilled cheese sandwiches.

"This is Mom's recipe," he said. "See, you put butter on the outside, Miracle Whip on the inside of one slice, then the cheese, then mustard. What do you think?"

"Nice," she said, being a good sport. "Maybe I'll make one like my mom made now." She made one her way and devoured it, leaving Pilate to wonder how she stayed so fit and trim.

After they finished, Pilate broke the silence. "So, do we have to say goodnight after this?"

"Afraid so. I have to pick up Kara by eleven," she said, her face a mock frown.

"Can I go with? I hate for you to drive alone on these roads at night," he said.

"Thanks, John, but it's probably best we don't just yet. I don't want to confuse Kara."

"Or upset Grif?"

"Well, I don't think he has anything against you, but he's protective of us."

"Hmm. Okay, but can I see you again soon?" He felt silly asking. They were office mates, after all.

"Let's just take it one day at a time," she said.

Pilate couldn't help but feel hurt by her answer, especially when Simon's laughter echoed in his mind like a bully mocking him for being picked last in gym. He nodded. "Of course."

She touched his cheek. "John, I came here tonight and... well, uh, spent this time with you because I like you, and I do want more from you, but I'm not so silly as to think you're going to stick around here very long."

"Well, I haven't really decided whether or not—"

"Exactly," she said.

"Wait...who says *you* are going to stick around here?" he said.

"Of course I'd like to go," she said, "but Grif would be all alone without us. I just can't."

"I understand," Pilate said, his stomach suddenly groaning. He felt a lump in his throat, and his eyes watered. *Jesus*, he said to himself. His emotions were out of control, swimming just under the surface. He felt a pain in his chest, the same one he'd felt when his mother had told him his granddad had died.

"John?" Kate said, her hand on his. "You okay?"

"Yeah, I'm fine. Must be an allergy or something," he said.

"An allergy?" she looked confused.

"Or maybe a vitamin deficiency," Pilate smiled. "Grilled cheese and cabernet aren't exactly packed with nutrients, you know."

She laughed. "Heh. Right."

Both jumped when the phone rang.

Pilate welcomed the distraction as he got up to answer it. "Hello?" he said.

"John, it's Sam."

"Oh, hi," he said, his knuckles scrubbing his scalp.

"Can we talk?"

Pilate watched Kate put their plates in the kitchen. "Now really isn't a good time," he said.

Kate leaned against the kitchen counter, watching him, with her arms folded against her chest.

"Sam, I have to go," he insisted.

"Bollocks. You aren't doing anything," she said. "I just want to talk, John. Please?"

"Samantha, I...I have a friend over."

She hung up.

Kate pulled on her boots.

"You're not going now, are you?" he said, sitting beside her.

"In a minute," she said. "Can I call Grif? I want to make sure Kara is ready when I get there."

He handed her the phone and felt an explanation was in order. "Hey, that was just—"

"None of my business," Kate said, taking the phone and dialing Grif's number.

He lit a cigarette.

Kate buttoned her shirt, holding the phone in the crook of her neck as she waited for Grif to answer, but he never picked up.

"No answer?"

She frowned. "Nope. But it's strange."

"What?"

"It's busy."

"Well, maybe he's tied up with something."

"He has several lines, though, and he never lets one ring off the hook. Hmm. I guess he's just busy with an intake."

"You want to wait a few minutes and call back?"

She shook her head.

"Well, let me go with you," he said.

"No, John. Thanks. I'm sure everything's fine." She stood. "I'll be okay." She took the cigarette from his hand, inhaled, and put it out. "Thanks for a wonderful night," she said, hugging him.

He kissed her neck.

She pulled away gently, smiled, and put on her coat.

"See you Monday," she said.

"Not if I see you first," he teased. "At least let me walk you to your car."

"No," she said. "Why should you risk catching a cold? I'm a big girl, John," she said with a reassuring smile, "and I've lived here long enough. I'll be fine."

Before John could protest further, the phone rang again.

She wrinkled her nose. "My, that Sam is persistent." She opened the door. "Goodnight."

He waved and watched her go as he picked up the phone. "Hello?" he said, irritated.

"Mr. Pilate? Morgan Scovill. Is Kate Nathaniel with you?"

"No, Sheriff, she isn't…but even if she were, I'd have to tell you it'd be none of your business."

"Can the ACLU bullshit," the sheriff said. "Look, we've, uh, had a little problem out at Grif Nathaniel's, and I need to get a hold of her."

"Grif's place? Oh God. Is Kara okay?"

"Yes, she's fine, but I really need to talk to Kate."

"She just left. Let me see if I can catch her," he said. "Hang on." Pilate dropped the phone on the couch where they had made love only moments before and sprinted outside. He found Kate scraping the ice off her windshield as the motor idled.

She whirled around and looked at Pilate, standing before her in his bare feet. "John? What is it? Did Samantha propose or something?" She smiled.

"Not exactly. Scovill's on the phone, Kate. He says, uh…"

"What is it, John? Spit it out," she said, looking stricken as she noticed the grim, worried expression on his face.

"He says something happened at Grif's."

In an instant, her expression changed from stricken to terrified, and she was speechless, letting the ice scraper fall to the ground as she mindlessly released it from her gloved grasp.

"Come inside, Kate. He's on the phone," Pilate said.

"No time," she said, and then she jerked open her car door. "Tell him I'm on my way," she said.

Pilate grabbed her arm and the car door. "No, Kate. You can't go until you talk to Scovill. Besides, I'm coming with you."

CHAPTER TWELVE

Pilate hastily pulled on his hiking boots, coat, and scarf as he watched Kate talk to Scovill on the phone.

"Is she all right? Well, what happened to Grif?" she said. "How? How bad?"

She hung up, and they hurried back to the idling car.

"I'll drive," he said.

She didn't argue.

As they wheeled onto the state road leading to Goss City, Pilate glanced at Kate. "What happened, Kate?" he asked.

"Grif's been beaten half to death," she said. "Scovill said County Memorial called Grif about eight saying they had an intake. Grif said that would be fine and he was ready. They brought the intake over around nine thirty and couldn't get an answer at the door or the phone of the mortuary. They tried the house and found Kara there asleep in front of the TV," Kate said, her voice shaking. "The driver asked Kara where her grandpa was, and she told them he went to the mortuary to take care of business. She knows the drill about Grif's business. Anyway, then she fell asleep until the driver knocked. The driver didn't want to alarm her, so he made her some chocolate milk and then called Scovill," she said. "John, please drive faster if you can."

"You got it." Pilate pressed the accelerator and passed a pickup. "What happened when Scovill got there?"

"He has a key, which is pretty normal, since the mortuary often doubles as a coroner's office in a little place like this. Scovill told the driver to stay with Kara. He went in and found Grif in the embalming room. He was…they beat him to a pulp. God. Poor Grif."

"Shit," Pilate said, pressing harder on the accelerator. "Is he…okay?"

"The driver took him back to County in the hearse," she said.

"Nice," Simon said in Pilate's head.

"He's in the emergency room," she said.

"Let's get Kara first," Pilate said.

When they rolled up on the mortuary, the lights from Sheriff Scovill's truck and a state trooper cruiser flashed brilliantly against the trees, house, and building. The few dejected stalks of a harvested cornfield behind the house played lonely witnesses in the moonlight.

Kate leapt out of the car almost before he had it in park and ran into the house.

Inside, Kara sat on the couch, talking with the state trooper as they shared a peanut butter and jelly sandwich.

Kate swept her little girl up into her arms. "Are you okay, honey?"

Kara nodded. "The policeman and I are having a PB and J while we wait for Grandpa," she said.

"Thank you, Officer," Kate said. "Honey, I think we will probably need to see Grandpa later, because…" She looked at the trooper.

"Because he's working late—you know, Kara, like we talked about before," he said. "The sheriff and I are just watching things while he's working."

She nodded and yawned. "Mommy, I'm tired."

"Let's go home, sweetie." Kate picked her up. "Thanks again, Officer. Uh, while I'm gathering Kara's things, would you mind telling my friend…uh, how late Kara's grandpa will be working?" She nodded her head at Pilate.

"Sure, ma'am."

When Kate and Kara were out of earshot, the trooper spoke. "Mr. Nathaniel took quite a beating in there," he said. "Sheriff Scovill found him on the floor of the embalming room. His face is a bloody mess, but we're sure he'll pull through."

"Any idea who did it? Or why?"

"Don't look like they took anything, though they rifled through the desk in his office," the trooper said. He was in his twenties, wearing a crew cut and a nametag that read "*Hulsey*." He flipped open a small, pocket-sized notebook. "The safe was open, and there was cash left in it. But again, nothing seemed to be missing."

"This kind of thing happen a lot around here?"

"Hell no," Hulsey snorted. "Scovill sounded pretty spooked when he called me on the radio."

"So you think Grif's okay?"

"Well, I meant to say he's stable, but long term, I couldn't say. He was semiconscious when Scovill got to him. I don't know what he said."

Kate walked back in with Kara's book bag flung over her shoulder and Kara hugging her neck. "John, we need to get Kara home," she said, the ease and comfort of their earlier lovemaking obliterated from her face. "Or do we need to go somewhere else?" she said, meaning the hospital.

"No. Everything is okay on that end," he said.

Kate looked relieved. "Good."

Heavy boots stamped on the front porch. The door opened after a couple of quick, cursory knocks, revealing Sheriff Scovill. He nodded to everyone. "Kate, he's fine. Go on home. We can talk about this tomorrow morning. I know you want to get Kara to bed," he said.

Kate nodded and walked past him to the door. She turned and looked at Scovill and Hulsey. "Thank you so much," she said.

"Trooper Hulsey is gonna follow you home, Kate."

Hulsey nodded and dutifully put on his hat and zipped his coat.

"Mr. Pilate, I could use your help, if you don't mind hanging back."

Pilate and Kate looked at Scovill, then back at each other. "It's okay, ma'am. I just need to ask him some questions."

"Morgan, John was...with me," Kate whispered, trying not to wake Kara.

Scovill looked at the floor. "I know, Kate, but I need to talk to him. I'll make sure he gets back to Cross okay."

Pilate smiled. "Go on home, Kate. We'll talk tomorrow."

Kate looked at Pilate, smiled weakly, and carried Kara to her car, Hulsey in tow.

Scovill glanced at Pilate, then out the window. "She's a special lady, Mr. Pilate."

"Yes, she is."

"She's had to take a lot of shit from people, what with her being so pretty."

"Really?"

"Yeah."

"What people?"

"Several. Lindstrom put the moves on her a while back."

"I see." Pilate's fists balled at his side. *Yet another reason why Lindstrom doesn't like me*, he thought.

"She handled him okay," Scovill said. "That girl shot him down in flames, just like the arrogant jackass deserved. It was funny as hell, if ya ask me."

"Good."

Scovill moved his head to the right at an odd angle, enough to make his neck pop. "Come on over to the mortuary and see what they did," he said.

"Sheriff..." Pilate said.

"Yup?"

"Isn't this a bit, uh...irregular? I mean, you're asking a civilian you hardly know to be a party to not one, but two crime scenes."

"Yes, it is irregular, but it ain't illegal or immoral, is it?"

"I suppose not."

"I'm a lawman, and I know not. Now come on."

Pilate wordlessly followed Scovill into the mortuary. They went through the lobby to Grif's office, which had clearly been ransacked.

"Man," Pilate said.

"It only gets better," Scovill said. "Come downstairs."

Scovill led Pilate to the door marked *"Private."* It opened into a room with filing cabinets, a small elevator just large enough for a gurney, and a door marked *"Authorized Personnel Only."* Scovill opened the door and went down some creaky wooden stairs that had been painted a sickly shade of green.

The odor of a cocktail of chemicals assaulted Pilate's nostrils. The room was poorly lit; the overhead lighting had apparently been smashed in the brawl earlier. Moonlight flooded in through three small basement windows lining the back wall.

Leaning against a piece of equipment that looked like something that would be used to remove bodily fluids, Scovill glanced at the arterial diagram pinned to the wall. He gestured at three prep tables. Two had bodies covered in white sheets, and the other was enclosed in a body bag; that bag presumably held the body of the night's new intake, a corpse from the nursing home whose arrival may have saved Grif Nathaniel's life.

"These are Mr. and Mrs. Nathaniel, whom I believe you have already met." Scovill walked away from the bodies toward a small desk. There were blood spatters all around it and on it, and crimson splotches on the paperwork that sat on its surface. "Looks like they beat hell out of Grif over here," Scovill said.

"They?"

"Well, well...a regular Jim Rockford, ain't ya?" Scovill said. "Yeah, I think it had to be at least a couple of guys. Grif didn't have any marks on his knuckles, so I'm sure somebody held him while the other one punched him. He couldn't fight back."

"Crap," Pilate said. "Why do you suppose they did it?"

"Robbery." Scovill said, monotone.

"Oh come on," Pilate said.

"You're right. Not robbery," Scovill said, bending over and using his ink pen to look under papers on the desk.

Pilate surveyed the room. "This has to have something to do with the crypt break in."

Scovill stood up straight, facing Pilate. "To think, you only have a master's degree in English lit. You'd be a hell of a criminologist."

"Thanks."

Scovill walked over to a closet door behind the desk and checked the knob; it was locked. He moved around the room, looking at shelves of embalming chemicals, mortician's wax, and other accoutrements of the trade.

"Mr. Pilate, if you were to wonder what the hell was going on—which I am sure you are—what would you think about all this?" He continued his orbit around the room, peering at the cold crematorium door.

Pilate cleared his throat. "Well, I'd have to think Grif Nathaniel is mixed up with some bad people."

"Now you're just irritating me," Scovill said. "Come on, college man. Spill it. What do you really think?"

"I think somebody must want something really bad—something they think Grif has. They want it bad enough to desecrate a grave, tear up a mortuary, and try to beat it out of him. I just wonder who that could be and what it is that they want."

"If you were to think about who those people might be, who would you suspect?"

"Who has the most to gain or lose from a secret Grif might be keeping?"

"Now you're getting somewhere," Scovill said. "The question is, did these people get what they were after?"

"Only Grif can answer that," Pilate said, folding his arms across his chest.

"True. Come on." Scovill hurried up the stairs and exited out the back door of the mortuary. Pilate followed him into the cold.

"What are you doing?"

Scovill surveyed the cornfield. "The hearse driver didn't pass anybody on the road when he came out here. I think our culprits walked here and back."

Pilate looked at the desolate field. "Through the cornfield?"

"Well, the road is the only way in for a vehicle." He pointed at the road and the lights of Goss City to the south.

"Going north, that road leads to Vetsville, about forty miles away. Goss City is a mile and a half the other direction. There're a couple creeks and several cattle fences that would make it tough to go that way unless they stuck to the highway, but it'd be nearly impossible to go that way unseen. That leaves the cornfield, about a two-mile hike to Cross as the crow flies."

"To Cross," Pilate repeated. "Can you see any tracks with your flashlight?"

"Nope. Too dark out here," he said, zipping his coat up closer to his neck against the cold. "I can look tomorrow."

"Okay," Pilate said. "Should we go talk to Grif?"

"Already did," Scovill said, looking back at the house.

"I thought he was incoherent," Pilate said.

"In a way, I almost wish he were," he said.

"What?"

Scovill turned around toward the door. "Come on. Let's get back inside."

The pair trudged back in.

Scovill unzipped his coat and sat down with a heavy sigh in the lobby, right under the painting of Martin Nathaniel.

"Mind if I smoke?" Pilate said, sitting opposite him and lighting up even before he had permission.

Scovill shrugged. "Mr. Pilate, there's a reason I asked you to stay. It's because of what Grif told me when I got here."

"Well, I thought it was odd of you, to say the least," he said, exhaling.

"When I found Grif, all he could get out was something about, 'They're going to kill Kate and Kara if they don't get it' or something like that, and then he passed out," he said.

"Jesus," Pilate said. "Who are these people?"

Scovill shook his head and took off his cap, sliding two fingers around the inside rim, his hand shaking.

Pilate pretended not to notice. "Well, Grif will have to tell us when he comes to," Pilate said.

"I get the strong impression that these people might also kill Kate and Kara if Grif I.D.s them," Scovill said.

Pilate stood up. "We need to go to Kate's...right now."

Scovill made a be-seated gesture with his shaky hand. "Trooper Hulsey is waiting there until Lenny can come over and watch them."

Pilate sat.

"Besides," Scovill added, "they won't mess with Kate and Kara either way. If they do, Grif most certainly won't cooperate."

"You're putting a lot of faith in these assholes, Sheriff," Pilate said.

"No, just logic," he said.

"Thanks, Spock, but I think you're forgetting that desperate people do desperate things. They seem to lack common sense and logic, don't you think?" Pilate said. He felt his face and ears reddening in anger.

"Calm down, Mr. Pilate. We have to keep our heads on straight," he said. "Tomorrow I'm going over to the hospital to talk to Grif. I will explain that he needs to let me in on some things."

"How much of this does Kate know?"

"Not much yet, but I'll tell her," he said.

"Let me," Pilate said. "I think I can talk her out of doing anything crazy."

"Kate isn't the type to go off the deep end, Pilate," Scovill said. "Just tell her what's happening and what we plan to do. Also, tell her also to leave this to us."

"Who's behind this?"

Scovill's eyes betrayed a flicker of thought. "I have an idea," he said.

"It's that goddamned land deal, isn't it?"

"Ah. You been talking to our local conspiracy buff, Derek Krall, huh?"

"So?"

"Well, I think the deal may have something to do with it, but I can't be sure until I talk to Grif," he said.

Pilate puffed on the cigarette a moment. "What now?"

"Well, I'm gonna lock up this here mortuary, run some crime scene tape around the front door, then take you to Kate's."

"Okay, but you have to keep me in the loop," Pilate said.

"That appears to be the plan," Scovill said.

CHAPTER THIRTEEN

Scovill dropped Pilate off at Kate's house in Cross. Deputy Lenny sat in his truck outside, the motor running. Pilate knocked on the door and was let in by Kate. She wore a heavy terrycloth bathrobe, and her hand rested on what looked to be a handgun in the robe pocket.

He hugged her tightly. She gestured for him to take a seat next to a corn-burning stove. The room was cozy; the faint aroma of roasted corn was a welcome change from the sickening smells of the embalming room.

"You okay?" he asked.

"Yes," she said, running a hand through her hair. "Kara's asleep in my room. Coffee?"

"No. It'll just make me want to smoke," he said, shaking his head.

"Go ahead. It'll add some variety to the popcorn smell," she said, rising to fetch the coffee. "Tell me what you know."

Pilate explained what he and Scovill had seen and what they thought.

"So we're in danger?" she said, her breath choppy.

"We really don't think so. They went after Grif because he has something they want. If they hurt you guys, they'll never get it. That's Scovill's thinking anyway."

Kate rolled her eyes. "I can't say I am terribly comforted by that," she said.

"Kate, Lenny and I are here. You're going to be fine," he said, sitting beside her. "We won't let anything happen to you or Kara."

She nodded, her eyes tearing.

He put his hand on her knee. "Kate, can you think of anything Grif might know that would make someone want to hurt him to get him to talk?"

"No. He's the sweetest man," she said. "He's suffered so much loss and pain in his life."

"I know," Pilate said, "but let's think here. What would make someone break into his parents' crypt looking for something and then beat him up? What does he have? What does he know?"

She shook her head. "I have no idea."

Pilate didn't want to agitate her. He leaned back on the couch, exhaling noisily. "Scovill's going to talk to Grif tomorrow."

"I'm going over in the morning," she said.

"Can I go?"

"You better," she said.

"Some date this turned out to be," Pilate snorted.

Kate slapped the side of his head and led him to the guest bedroom.

When they arrived at the county hospital Saturday morning, Doc Hutton apologetically informed them that they had put Grif in a Diprivan-induced coma to give him a better chance to fight the swelling and damage he'd sustained in the beating.

"This is a good thing," Hutton said. "It really can help the body concentrate on healing itself."

"May I see him?" Kate asked.

Pilate sat with Kara in the waiting room, looking at old magazines while Kate visited Grif.

"Is Grandpa going to be okay?" Kara said, closing a dog-eared issue of *Highlights*.

"You bet," Pilate said. "The doctors are gonna make him all better."

"Good. He's my only grandpa," she said, resting her head on Pilate's shoulder.

"I know, sweetheart." He stroked her hair. "I know."

Kate dropped Pilate off and headed home. She and Kara needed to sleep.

Lenny had moved on at daybreak. He would be back to watch the house at nightfall.

Pilate made himself a cup of coffee, dumped several heaping spoons of sugar in it, lit a cigarette, and sat on his living room floor. He shuffled through the stack of papers about the Bernard murders and reread several pages rapidly.

His eyes danced over dozens of lines on several pages until he found what he was looking for: the one fact about the Bernard murder that put it all together.

"That's got to be it," Pilate said to himself. "It's fucking got to be."

Pilate's car was still in Jimmy's garage, but he really wanted to have a look around the cornfield behind Grif's place, and he didn't need any companions. His gut told him Scovill was a trustworthy sort, but he also knew that Scovill's father had played an important role in that situation all those years ago. That meant Scovill could be in on the whole thing, and if that was the case, Kate and Kara really were in danger. In an attempt to obey the better-to-be-safe- than-sorry rule, Pilate had to consider Morgan Scovill untrustworthy and keep an eye on him.

He slept fitfully, rising early Sunday morning to the sound of church bells. He contemplated trying to get Jimmy to release his car from the garage, but he knew that would be a fool's errand on a Sunday. Krall had mentioned before that Jimmy considered Sundays holy in his own way: The mechanic celebrated the Sabbath by enjoying a case of beer in front of the tube.

So, Pilate made his regular Sunday call to his parents, careful not to worry them with anything beyond the events at work. His mother filled him in on family gossip and his father on the latest news of the long-storied plant closing.

Just before he said goodbye, his mother took the phone back from Pilate's father. "Johnny," she said, choosing the tone she always reserved for her most motherly moments. "What's wrong?" "Nothing, Mom," he lied, fighting the urge to spill his guts.

"I'm fine."

"You're not," she said. "Are you taking your vitamins?" her pet name for his antidepressants whenever she mentioned them in front of Pilate's father, for talk of his son taking antidepressants always made John's dad uncomfortable.

"Yeah, Mom."

"Johnny, do you need to come home?"

"Yes," he wanted to say. *"I'm in over my head here. It's like when I went away to camp when I was ten. I cried every day because I wanted to come home and read books and just be left alone, except here there are bad people doing bad things, Mommy, and it's dangerous!"* Instead, he could only answer, "Mom, I'm fine—just the usual fitting in and new job issues, you know?"

His mother paused. "All right, Johnny, but if you decide you want to come home, we're here for you."

"I know, Mom. I know, and I appreciate it."

CHAPTER FOURTEEN

By three o'clock, he'd checked the temperature on the old thermometer screwed into the wall outside. It was a partly sunny forty degrees, and he decided it would be okay to hike it.

Pilate rummaged through his kitchen junk drawer and found his Swiss Army knife, a small flashlight, and a glasscutter Samantha had once used to make stained glass Christmas ornaments. He dug in his closet until he found a mini survival kit in a plastic jug, something he'd gotten for Christmas the previous year. He grabbed a couple of granola bars and a half-liter of bottled water and shoved it all in his beat-up leather backpack.

He donned long underwear, jeans, hiking boots, and a sweatshirt. He put on his wool pea coat, threw the backpack over one shoulder, and walked out the door into the sunlight. The January sun reflected off partially melted patches of ice and snow. He slipped his sunglasses on and walked down the street toward the soy and cornfields that rimmed the edge of town on the way to Goss City.

He had to walk past a few houses on his way there; the carillon bells played show tunes. Within a few blocks he was warm under his coat and began to wish he had not worn the long johns.

After about fifteen minutes, he reached the main road leading out of Cross. Once he crossed over that and into the fields, he knew he would be hard to detect, unless someone was watching the fields.

As he reached the road, a familiar luxury SUV stopped beside him. The passenger window rolled down, revealing Jack Lindstrom, his catalog store driving gloves gripping the wheel. "Need a ride?" he said, his tone pleasant, though his eyes were as cold as ever.

"Oh, no, sir. Thanks," Pilate said. "I'm just out taking a hike, trying to get some fresh air."

Lindstrom eyed his backpack. "Hiking? In January? In this weather?"

"Not so bad," Pilate said, cringing at his breath, which was visible in the cold as he spoke. He glanced in the back seat of Lindstrom's SUV. Several rolls of what appeared to be architectural plans were strewn across it.

"Uh-huh," Lindstrom said.

The SUV engine idled as the two men looked at each other's faces.

"So, I hear you've been seeing Kate Nathaniel." Lindstrom's eyes narrowed.

Pilate just looked back at Lindstrom.

"Well, anyway, enjoy your hike."

"Will do," Pilate said, taking a step back from the vehicle as the window went back up.

Then, suddenly, the window stopped in its tracks and rolled back down. "Oh...and Mr. Pilate..."

"Yes, Dr. Lindstrom?"

"Your contract is not going to be renewed," he said, smiling. "We don't need you. I just thought you'd like to know so you can plan your summer. Trevathan will give you the paperwork."

Pilate didn't bother saying another word to the man, as he had nothing else to say—at least nothing he could say.

Lindstrom's power window rose, and the SUV slowly pulled away.

"And fuck you very much," Pilate said.

He strode toward the field, his boots crunching the cold earth within a minute or two. As he walked, Pilate saw several small yellow surveyors' flags placed a few yards apart here and there. "Shit," he said. *This was Bartley's land—the land that was meant to be sold to the wilier of the town's biggest bastards. All this for a land deal?*

"Forget it, John. It's Chinatown." Simon's voice echoed in his head.

Pilate soldiered on, crossing from a field into a small grove of trees in a small valley. A massive oak tree and several smaller maples constituted the grove, which hid a hunter's deer stand about ten feet off the ground.

He climbed up into the stand and sat under the camouflage netting amidst several empty beer cans and beef jerky wrappers.

Pilate peered out the gun slits in the deer stand, viewing nothing but empty fields. A cloud front was coming in from the north, but it didn't look too threatening to anything but the sunshine.

"Well, John, congratulations! You got your ass fired," the singsong voice of Simon pierced the silence. *"This has to be a new record for you."*

"Not now," Pilate said.

"And just what the hell are you doing out here? Trespassing, playing commando and Columbo all at the same time? Really, John. It's kind of pathetic, don't you think? Who do you think you are?"

Pilate suddenly felt a terrific pain behind his eyes. He rubbed his temples and lit a cigarette, then squeezed his eyes closed.

He sat for a peaceful moment, sensing nothing but the breeze in his ears and smoke in his lungs.

Simon cleared his throat, as if he was tired of being ignored. *"Still here."*

Pilate opened his eyes and saw Simon's shape under the netting in the opposite corner of the cramped deer stand.

"Why not end this? Permanently escape this vale of tears? Shuffle off this mortal coil? Take the dirt nap?" Simon said. *"How long can you*

keep this up anyway?" the specter tempted. *"Will Kate want anything to do with you when she finds out you got canned?"*

"Fuck off."

"Or will it be when she finds out that you're a tad mental and too stubborn or too stupid to take your medication?" Simon shifted under the net. *"Then again, maybe she'll just get killed because you and these hicks have no idea how to protect her, you worthless piece of—"*

Pilate lunged at the shape under the net, a loud *crack* signifying the side of the deer stand giving way. He fell ten feet and landed hard on the frozen ground with his backpack under him. The plastic survival kit case made a cracking sound as the wind escaped Pilate's lungs.

His eyes opened into cautious slits. The world was vertical, though his field of vision was horizontal. Pilate mentally inventoried his bones, testing his arms and legs for pain or fractures; nothing was broken, as far as he could discern.

Something moved past his field of vision a few yards away. An undernourished doe gingerly padded around, looking for food.

Pilate laughed, spooking the deer back into the recesses of the grove. "Run, Bambi, run," he said weakly, sitting up.

He had been unconscious for only a minute or two, but it was long enough that the clouds now eclipsed the sun. He looked at his watch. *Four thirty? Already? I have to get moving.*

Pulling himself up on his haunches, he felt his back pop; it felt good. He checked the contents of his bag and found the survival kit case cracked in pieces, its contents spilled loosely all over the bottom of his bag: waterproof matches, a surprisingly unbroken mirror, compass, flint, needle, thread, and bandages.

He opened the water and gulped down half of it. Then, standing gingerly to his feet, he took a moment to get his bearings. Once he had regained his composure a bit, he headed again toward the highway and the back way into Nathaniel's Mortuary.

An hour later, after a few wrong turns and ripping a two-inch hole in his pants on some barbed wire, Pilate spied the Nathaniel place from his terraced hilltop perch. There were no cars around and not much Sunday traffic passing on the state highway in front. It was never exactly a traffic jam anyway.

His watch read five fifteen, and the sunrays were making their last stand. It was colder, too, and the long johns seemed now a brilliant bit of planning. He crouched and headed down the terraced hill into a small line of trees that grew like a planned perimeter around the cornfield that guarded the back of the mortuary.

Pilate did his best seen-it-in-the-movies stealth routine as he navigated in the twilight through the cornfields. He felt scared, exhilarated, and more than a little idiotic.

An owl hooted just as he made it to the side door of the mortuary that he and Scovill had exited the day before. Pilate thought of his old college roommate, Brian, a U.S. Army paratrooper before college. When Pilate had asked Brian what it felt like to jump out of an airplane, Brian had said, "Oh it's fine. A little squirt of piss runs down your leg, and then you're okay." The hoot of that owl had given Pilate his first squirt-of-piss experience, and to his surprise, just like Brian said, once that was over, he was, in fact, okay.

He put a gloved hand on the doorknob and turned, but it was locked, just as he expected. What he was counting on was getting in one of the three basement windows along the back of the building. He hoped he could manage to open one, and that it would be big enough for him to squeeze through.

Pilate knelt beside the one closest to the door, fishing around in his backpack for the flashlight. He shone it into his backpack until he found the glasscutter, quickly identified the location of the lock on the window, turned off the light, and applied the glasscutter to the pane. He tried to cut a half-moon shape large enough for his hand, but the old glass wouldn't cut. In fact, the stupid glasscutter barely made a mark. Cary Grant in *To Catch a Thief* he was not. Pilate slipped the useless glasscutter in his coat pocket and punched the glass.

The entire window shattered.

"Shit."

Listening for signs of alarm and hearing nothing, Pilate punched out a few more shards of glass and dropped his bag inside. It made a loud *thump* on the floor below. He backed his legs inside the window. His hips went in without a hitch, but his bulky pea coat bunched up around the doorframe.

Crap.

He wriggled, gravity pulling him further until the coat was around his ears. He pushed against the ground and fell inside, landing badly on his feet, his right ankle popping—and not in the feel-good way like his back had after his plummet from the deer stand. "Ow!" he said in spite of himself.

He tested his weight on the ankle. It was okay for the time being, but he figured it would be complaining in the morning. Pilate felt around on the floor for his backpack, then removed the flashlight. He clicked it on and waited for his eyes to adjust.

The small light beam diffused at about three feet as he carefully crept toward the center of the room, glass from the shattered overhead lights crunching underfoot like rock candy. The small, blood- spattered desk came into view, and the bodies of Martin and Millie Nathaniel were lying sentinel just a few feet away.

The third table was bare; the body from the nursing home had been carted off to the funeral home in Vetsville, he supposed, unless it was in the freezer, and he wasn't curious enough to look.

He felt like *Kolchak: The Night Stalker,* minus the seersucker suit and tennis shoes. His mother loved that show almost as much as she loved *Columbo.* Pilate wondered what she would think of what he was doing in that minute and if she'd think him anything like Peter Falk.

Acclimated to the layout of the room, Pilate pointed the light back to the desk. Behind it was the locked closet Scovill had left alone when they'd examined the crime scene the night before.

Pilate inched carefully across the room, careful not to disturb anything. He tried the door of the closet, but it was still locked. He retraced his steps back to the desk. He had to find something to force the lock.

He opened the center drawer of the desk, looking for a letter opener or screwdriver. He found one with a large, ornate Goss City Kiwanis logo on the end. He picked it up, revealing a brass key attached to a large paperclip. He quickly took the key, went over to the door, and slid it into the lock. He gave the knob a turn, and the door opened with a loud *creak*.

Pilate felt an emotion akin to winning a slot machine jackpot. He quickly entered the walk-in closet and closed the door. He banged his head on the single light bulb dangling in the center of the room. He pulled the chain on the light, and his pupils contracted painfully.

Once his eyes adjusted, he spied several wall-to-wall shelves, each full of cardboard boxes and bottles of chemicals. He removed a sheet from a stack of new white sheets and tucked it under the door to block any light that might escape the sixty-watt bulb swinging from the ceiling.

Pilate turned his attention to the shelving. Working left to right, he quickly read the labels on pedestrian boxes marked *"Perfect Tone"* and *"Eotone."* Then he moved past those to boxes of mortician's wax and a box marked *"Professional's Choice Cosmetic Kit."*

Pilate examined older-looking boxes on the top shelf. Some were stuffed with paperwork. One contained Christmas decorations recently packed away after the last holiday. Pilate started to replace the box when he noticed a cardboard cylinder unceremoniously shoved behind a couple of bottles of red liquid marked *"B&G Lyf-Lyk Tints."* Standing on his tiptoes, Pilate reached for the cylinder. His fingertips grazed it, but it was too far back to grasp.

He looked around in the small closet and found a stepladder tucked between two of the shelves. He set it up and climbed to the third rung. Grunting, Pilate reached into the dark recesses of the shelf. An outraged spider crawled up his hand, and the teacher jerked his hand back, shaking the spider off. "That's all I need. A black widow bite," he said under his breath. He reached back in and grasped the cylinder with both hands, gently drawing it out.

In the light, a dark dust that was actually soot covered the heavy cardboard cylinder. He wiped away the soot that coated a desiccated label glued to the top and could finally read, "*Brady Floyd Bernard, 1909-1963.*"

J. ALEXANDER GREENWOOD

CHAPTER FIFTEEN

Pilate sat on the step ladder, holding Brady Bernard in his hands. He turned the surprisingly heavy, soot-covered cylinder over, the ashes rolling around inside like a tragic hourglass.

Ironically, the ashes had survived the fire a few years prior, and the tornado as well. He simply had to open the cylinder. It was his grail—holy or not—the reason he'd ventured there. For a moment, he considered that what he was doing was really no better than what those thugs had done to Martin and Millie's crypt.

But I...I have to. For Kate and Kara. Perhaps for my own sanity. I have to be right about something. I have to...to do what's right.

He set the cylinder down, opened his Swiss Army knife, and carefully cut the heavy tape wound around the center of the cylinder; it cut away easily. He pulled the top off the cylinder with a *whoosh*, the sound like that of opening a poster mailing tube, and Bernard's ashes rushed back into the world for the first time in more than forty years. Pilate turned his head and covered his mouth to avoid inhaling what was left of the man.

Waving a hand in front of him, he turned on his flashlight and shone it inside the cylinder. Inside, amidst what looked like the remains of a campfire, lay a small brown book. Pilate retrieved it and discovered that the book was actually a ledger, held together with a dried-out, fat rubber band. He gently brushed ashes off the book and laid it on a shelf.

He shook the cylinder gently from side to side to see if there was anything else hidden amongst Brady Bernard's mortal remains; he found nothing other than large roasted bone chips and ash. "Sorry, Brady," he felt obliged to whisper.

Pilate resealed the cylinder and put it back on the shelf where he'd found it, carefully camouflaging it with the bottles and boxes that had obscured it before.

He tucked the ledger in the breast pocket of his pea coat and quickly put the room back together the way he'd found it.

Pilate pulled the chain on the light bulb, slung his book bag over his shoulder, and opened the closet door.

The two dead bodies silently witnessed him pick up the desk chair and place it under the window. *Dead men—and women—tell no tales,* he had to remind himself as he stepped on cracked glass, wincing at the sound as he mounted the chair to pull himself through the window. He threw his backpack outside, double-checked that the ledger was secure in his breast pocket and made his escape.

The cold air slapped his face. The temperature had fallen by at least ten degrees, and to his dismay, Pilate saw fat snowflakes coating the ground. *They'll know,* he thought, sickened by the catastrophic coincidence of show falling at just that moment. *They'll recognize my boot prints.*

After he had made it out the window, he cursed and looked around. Feeling exposed, he ran through the snowy cornfield, up the hill and back toward the scarce lights of Cross. The snow was falling in threatening flurries, obscuring his vision and forcing him to leave a mark that he didn't want to leave. His lungs burned from exertion. He wondered if his shattered survival kit had anything that might keep him from getting lost in the snow.

Stumbling in the dark, Pilate fell hard on his right knee and tripped into a small gulley. Cursing, he rubbed his knee, climbed out of the gulley, and continued on, a limp interrupting his gait.

He made it back to the grove and deer stand, which provided him some shelter from the snowfall, like a tiny awning. Headlights from the county road nearby came and went. Pilate checked his watch: seven thirty. He'd been out there a long time, and the snow was falling harder and harder. It was a consolation, though, because if enough fell, it would cover his tracks and leave him untraceable to anyone investigating the mortuary break-in.

Pilate wondered if Scovill would consider him a suspect. Thinking back to the broken glass, he remembered the glasscutter in his pocket. He wiped it off carefully of fingerprints and then used his gloved hand to toss it as far away as he could into the snowy abyss.

As he sat there in the dark, the moon quickly becoming obscured by clouds and snow, he felt as vulnerable and alone as he had in a very long time. Standing in a grove of trees that broke up a soybean field, his teeth chattering, Pilate almost wished he could take it all back, make it un-happen. *I'm not sure I can do this,* he second-guessed himself. *Maybe he's right. Who do I think I am?*

He removed his gloves, laid them on his lap, then fished in his pockets for his lighter and cigarettes. He lit one, then replaced the pack and lighter. Pilate wanted to remove the small ledger from his pocket to study it in the flickering glow of the tip of his cigarette, but he couldn't risk getting it wet in the snow. *I just need to finish the damn cigarette and get back to Cross. Kate might be looking for me.*

Pilate smoked the cig halfway, put it out in the snow, and lumbered to his feet, his knee groaning. He looked down for a moment, feeling a little lightheaded. He was hungry, and he decided in that moment that nothing would be better than a heated-up can of Dinty Moore beef stew. It was good bachelor chow, something Kolchak might eat after a night of ghost busting.

Pilate walked a few steps from the deer stand and then went back. Flicking on his flashlight, he found the cigarette butt he'd just extinguished and put it in his pocket.

He managed to slip into Cross without being seen. He saw no cars on the road; most students were away for the weekend, likely putting off any return plans until the snow had been plowed, which could take days in a place like that.

Dodging main streets and sticking to alleys, Pilate finally managed to get into his apartment around nine p.m. He stripped off his clothes, tossed them in the hamper, and threw his potentially incriminating boots in the back of his closet.

He draped the pea coat over an old kitchen chair he'd rescued from a curbside trash pickup a few days prior.

Chilled and hungry, Pilate opened the can of stew he'd been fantasizing about during his cold journey. It looked a lot like dog food, but he yearned for it nonetheless. He dumped it in a pan and turned on the range. A check of his phone revealed that Kate had indeed called a couple of hours earlier, but she hadn't left a message. He went to the bathroom, took off the long johns, and stepped into a scalding shower.

His knee was tender and already bruising from the fall he'd taken in the gulley, and his ankle was stiff, but neither was too painful unless he put all his weight on them. He slipped on some sweatpants and a Cross College sweatshirt, ran a comb through his hair, and went to the kitchen.

The aroma of the dog food-looking stew made his stomach growl. *Bachelors can't be choosy,* he mused as he stirred the chunks of alleged beef around in the gravy and mushy vegetables, then ladled the stew into a chipped bowl. He slathered some bread with margarine, poured a glass of milk, and sat down to eat.

Pilate polished off the stew, bread, and milk in less than five minutes. He put the dishes in the sink and was reaching for the ledger in his coat pocket when a loud knock on the door shattered his peace.

He went to the door, trying not to limp. He looked out a small window by the door and saw the unmistakable shape of

Sheriff Scovill standing there. *Der Komissar's in town. Uh-oh.* Wincing mentally, he opened the door. "Sheriff? Come in, come in," he said, trying to sound more hospitable than suspicious. "Is Kate all right? What?"

Scovill stamped his feet and removed his hat. His squinty eye regarded Pilate's sweatpants, shirt, and wet hair. "She's fine," he said. "Haven't you talked to her?"

Pilate gestured for the sheriff to have a seat on the couch. "Not since earlier today. She and Kara were pretty tired, and I thought I would let them get some rest. I was kind of tired myself."

"Do you always shower at night?"

"Um, no," Pilate said, reaching for a cigarette, "but I didn't shower this morning and felt a little scummy. Didn't want to go to bed without cleaning up."

Scovill nodded. "So after the hospital today you just came home?"

"Yup," Pilate said, quickly changing the subject. "I guess you heard they induced a coma for Grif," he said, lighting a cigarette.

"Yep. I just checked, and he's still under," Scovill said. "Now I guess all we can do is wait and see."

"Well, as frustrating as it is, that is probably the best thing for Grif right now," Pilate said.

"Strange days."

"No doubt." Scovill sat still for a moment, regarding Pilate. "Sheriff, did you come here just to interrogate me about my bathing habits, or is there something else I can help you with?"

"Well," he said, "I really came to ask if you've given anymore thought to why Grif got banged up."

"I'm at a loss, other than the fact that Grif must have something that somebody else is willing to go to macabre lengths to obtain," Pilate said.

"Have something or knows something," Scovill added.

"Well, yeah."

"So anyway…" Scovill stood up. "We may get eight inches tonight. We may have to close school Monday if we can't get the salt trucks and scrapers moving."

Pilate also stood. "Well, I wouldn't complain. I could use a day off."

"What, after lying around here all day eatin' dog food and smelling scummy?" Scovill said.

"Well, actually, Sheriff, I did take a walk around town this afternoon, so I'm a little worn out."

"I see. Cold day for a walk though," he said, looking past Pilate at the pea coat on the chair.

"Well, I needed some air. Needed to clear my head."

Scovill put on his hat. "Understandable." He went to the door. "If I figure anything out or think of anything, I'll call you," Pilate said.

Scovill's squint regarded Pilate. "You do that." He went back into the snow as Pilate closed the door behind him.

Pilate watched Scovill's truck pull away through the snow. He crossed the room to the pea coat, which was damp and glistening from the melted snow on the shoulders. He retrieved the ledger from the pocket. He blew some ash from it and dusted it off with a paper towel. He then put the paper towel, which had bits of Brady Bernard on it, aside. He would flush it later. The fat rubber band broke when he tugged it. He put that aside, too, and then opened the pages.

Inside was a standard, lined business ledger with numerous entries of numbers next to various initials like "O.O.", "M.N.", "J.S." and several others. It could be a gambling book, for all Pilate could tell. Of more interest were the scraps of paper tucked between the pages. Many of the yellowing pieces of paper also contained numbers and letters. In the back of the ledger, tucked between the last page and the back cover, was a neatly typed letter:

Dear Marty,

Well, by now you have this letter, so you know what I did…and I guess you have a good idea why. Wally should have just left me alone. After all my years at Cross, I deserved to stay.

So, after I write this, I am tucking it in my jockey shorts, because I know it will be you who will find it when you prepare me for the funeral. No need for an autopsy since it's clear how I ended this, so Dr. Tandy won't have any need to look in my drawers.

First off, there's a ledger I stole from that jackass Olafson. He never could keep his mouth shut when he was drinking, and when he fucked my wife, he talked too damn much. She told me everything before I kicked her cheating, two-faced ass out of my house.

The ledger is an accounting of all the money he was getting from his black market car racket.

It's all in there—cars stolen by Negro kids in the city who drove them out here to the sticks and passed them on to Olafson's son. Ollie Jr. stripped them down and sold the parts. Scovill gave them cover and made sure parts they couldn't sell ended up at the bottom of the river by Patterson Point. There's also a Negro boy chained inside a stolen '57 Chevrolet at the bottom of the river. He got crossways with Olafson's thug namesake last year.

I figured I ought to tell you about this, since you're a decent fellow and I know you'll tell the state patrol since we can be assured our beloved sheriff will cover it up.

Anyway, don't judge me too harshly for what I've done. Wally and Gareth were supposed to be my friends. I guess a white man really does skin his friends.

Warmly, Brady

"God," Pilate said, putting the pieces together. *So Bernard killed his bosses for firing him and tried to take down the guy who screwed his wife on the way out. Something went wrong though. Martin Nathaniel got scared and never revealed what he knew— that our current Mayor Olafson, as a young man, under orders from his father, murdered one of his car thief conspirators.* "Whoa," Pilate said. He read the bizarre letter again and again.

He pondered whether he should call Kate and tell her. *She might go off half-cocked. Besides, this implicates Scovill's father.*

That puts the sheriff in the untrustworthy category for good, as far as I'm concerned.

He picked up the phone. "Krall? John Pilate. We need to talk."

"Okay." Krall sounded tired and hung over.

"I gotta come over," Pilate said. "John, can't this wait? It's not a night fit for man or beast," he said.

"Can't do this over the phone, Krall."

Pilate heard a muffled sound on the receiver, as if Krall were covering the phone so he could speak to someone without Pilate hearing. "Okay, John. You got any snowshoes?"

"I'll manage," Pilate said.

Pilate trudged the half-mile or so to Krall's ramshackle Victorian pile on the east side of Cross. Snow covered the flaking paint and pathetic rock garden that was a favorite receptacle for students' empty beer cans, tossed from cars. Knocking the snow off his boots, Pilate saw two sets of tracks leading away from the porch into the street. He didn't have to knock, as Krall was standing in the doorway, watching for his approach.

"Lo and behold, the human icicle!" Krall bellowed.

Pilate brushed past.

Krall closed the door behind him. "Here. This'll warm your bones."

Accepting the brandy, Pilate sipped it before taking off his coat, and then he took a seat beside the fireplace. "Thanks. I needed that," he said.

"On the house," Krall said, plopping down on an overstuffed couch that served as a resting place for stacks of newspaper, magazines, and at least three books all lying spine up. "So, what's all the late-night mid-blizzard commotion about?"

Pilate explained, between a few of Krall's interruptions, what had happened. When he got to the part about breaking into the mortuary, he stopped. "Anyway, I found this." He produced the ledger and the letter and handed it to Krall.

Krall took the items and immediately read the letter. His mouth moved in spots as he read, his face a roadmap of surprise and excitement. He let out a long, low whistle and set the letter down on the coffee table between them. "Jesus."

Pilate nodded. "Do you mind?" He held up a cigarette.

Krall waved at him in assent. "John, this is quite an artifact."

"Yes, it answers a lot of questions," Pilate said, exhaling his smoke into the fireplace.

"It would seem so," Krall said, his fingers steepled together before his face. "But why now? What's going on here that is making Olafson want to find this now? I mean, how would he know it even exists?"

"Not sure. I mean, certainly he can read, and the historical documents state that Martin Nathaniel last had possession of Bernard's ashes and no one had claimed them, but surely they would have gone after them sooner than this."

"Well, that fire that took out the mortuary a few years ago was pretty suspicious. Sheriff Scovill Sr. signed off on it as being a lightning strike, but that seems to be a pretty lame excuse to me," Krall said.

"Exactly. Maybe they thought they'd knock out any evidence with a fire," Pilate said. "But what I still go back to is, why now?"

"Somebody…" Krall paused a moment, looking at the fire. "Somebody musta stirred up some shit. Somebody must've done something to get ol' Ollie thinking he's on the spot and about to be dropped in the grease."

"But who? And why?

"Think, Professor. The land deal." Krall smacked his hands together. "Who is the only one standing between Ollie and his golf course dreams?"

"Lindstrom!" Pilate said. "Shit. So you think he started mouthing off? But how would he know anything?"

"Shit, John. He doesn't, but he's heard the rumors, and Lindstrom may have done some digging. I mean, everyone in town thinks there's something suspicious about Marty Nathaniel's death." He scratched absently at his ear. "You put the right rumors in the wrong ears, and people have a tendency to get nervous— especially if they have something to hide."

"Brilliant. Lindstrom played them," Pilate said, lighting another cigarette.

"Gimme," Krall said, snatching the cig away and puffing on it. "You don't smoke," Pilate said.

"I know," Krall said, sucking on the cigarette.

"Lindstrom knows Ollie has ties to the Klan and God knows what else," Pilate said. "From what I hear, the Klan ruled around here until the eighties."

"The eighties? For shit's sake, Pilate, they still do," Krall said, hopping up to retrieve a book off a shelf.

"There's no Klan anymore," Pilate said. "Just the NRA."

"They may not call themselves Klan, but the guys who were in the KKK are still running things in this town. Look." Krall opened a Cross Public School yearbook and pointed at a photo of several young men with the words *"Cross Cavaliers"* printed above it.

"What the hell were the Cross Cavaliers?" Pilate said.

"You mean *Klavaliers,* a social club," he said, making air quotes. "They helped keep the community clean…and I'm not talking about picking up litter. They kept everything white and pure and clean, if you know what I'm saying."

"I get it," Pilate said. "KKK."

Krall stabbed at the photo with his bony finger. "Yeah but look at the members."

Pilate looked at the faces and then read the caption. "Some of these names are familiar…Olafson, Mostek, Kennedy…Nathaniel. Oh my God! That's Grif Nathaniel with Ollie Jr. Shit, Krall. What are we on to here?"

"I don't know, but it's something." Krall closed the yearbook. "They were all tight back then. Looks like something really bad happened and Marty and Grif got a bad case of the shakes."

"Or developed a conscience," Pilate said.

"Right. You freaking liberals," Krall snorted. "You're all so damn trusting of the good in people."

"Krall, do you think Scovill knows about this?"

"I really don't know," he said. "Morgan's a decent fella, and I would really hate to think he'd cover anything up. Then again, the memory of his father is important to him. His dad died of diabetes a few years back, and Morgan just idolized that man. When he got elected sheriff three years ago like Daddy dearest, it was the proudest moment of his life."

"But I have to tell the law about this," Pilate said. "I need to call the FBI or the state police."

"Whoa, tiger. Wait," Krall said, holding his hands up. "This is all conjecture, John. We can't do this. It would stir a huge shit storm and get us fired."

Pilate looked at his lap. "Too late for that on my end. My pink slip's already been signed."

"What? They fired you already?"

"I ran into Lindstrom on my way to the mortuary. He was kind enough to stop his car and tell me I'm being let go at the end of semester." Pilate flicked his cigarette butt into the fire.

"Well, there you have it." Krall leaned back, covering his face with his hands. He sighed deeply, then leaned forward. "The semester ends in a couple months. You stay out of trouble until then, and then you go and forget this place ever existed."

"Fuck no," Pilate said. "Besides the fact that we ought to do the right thing, you're forgetting Kate and Kara. I can't just stand by and let this happen. It might endanger them."

"What are you going to do? Tell Kara that her grandfather is an accessory to the murder of a Negro boy chained inside a '57 Chevy at the bottom of the Missouri River? Is that what you want Kara to know?"

Pilate stood up, and his knee popped. "Ouch."

"John, you're also forgetting that you broke into the mortuary to get this evidence. Scovill will nail you to the wall for breaking and entering and tampering with a police investigation. Hell, they might even say you planted it."

Pilate's stomach lurched.

"You're in a very bad spot, my friend," Krall said.

"I know," Pilate said, "but this is wrong. Something needs to be done."

"Maybe so, but that doesn't mean it has to involve you. Look, John, you're a good man, and if you stick your nose in this, all you'll be doing is getting yourself in hot water, embarrassing Kate's family, and giving Jack Lindstrom the land he needs to build that fucking shrine to himself—and that's only if you're lucky and that Cro-Mag Mayor Bounderby doesn't decide to have you killed. You don't wanna be seat belted into a watery grave yourself, do ya?"

Pilate hurried to the front door. He was sweating from the fireplace and didn't feel well. He stepped out to the porch railing and threw up.

Krall stood in the doorway. "You okay?"

Pilate shook his head, and when he threw up again, the Dinty Moore strangely looked the same as it had going in.

"Thanks for that," Krall said. He went to the kitchen and fetched Pilate a glass of water.

Pilate sipped the water slowly as he sat on the couch, turned away from the fire.

"John, buddy, you gotta keep this under your hat," Krall said.

"I'll think about it," Pilate said.

"Like hell you will." Krall snatched the letter and ledger and threw them into the fireplace.

"What the hell?"

"Sorry, buddy, but it's for your own good."

CHAPTER SIXTEEN

Pilate thrust his hands into the fire. His hair burned and his skin seared as he snatched the ledger and the letter it loosely protected inside from the flames. "Damn it, Krall, you son of a bitch," he said.

"I'm sorry, John. I just don't want anything bad to happen," Krall said.

Throwing on his coat, Pilate glared at Krall. "In case you haven't noticed, bad things are already happening, you jackass. And need I remind you that it was *you* who got me interested in all this shit in the first place?"

"I know, John, but it's all out of control now," Krall said, his voice shaky. "It wasn't supposed to go down like this."

Pilate didn't hear the last sentence from Krall as he slammed the door behind him and trudged out into the snowy darkness. He needed to get the ledger and letter somewhere safe, but Kate's was out of the question. He didn't want anyone to find her with it.

Krall watched Pilate angrily trudge away. "Poor bastard," he said under his breath. Then he pushed the curtain back in place and gazed into the fire.

He poured a scotch into a chipped coffee mug, gulped down half of it, and then picked up the phone. Falling gracelessly on his couch, sending an avalanche of newspapers and books sliding to the floor, he dialed.

"Hi. It's me," he said. "Look, um…I think we got a problem." Krall nervously pawed at his scalp with one hand as he talked on the phone.

"Well, he figured it out." He paused, listening. "I have no idea…uh-huh…smarter than he looks I guess."

Krall fidgeted some more with his hair as he listened.

"No, I most certainly did not! He broke in there and found it. Yes, there really is something to it. How was I supposed to know…Scovill? I can't tell."

Krall listened for about three more minutes before he had a break in the conversation in which to retort.

"Look, for all I know, it *was* all bullshit, but now the whole thing is getting out of hand. You know what happened to Grif Nathaniel, and you were seen there yourself…no, no, I am not saying you had anything to do with that, but this is becoming—"

The person on the other end of the line shouted, forcing Krall to hold the phone from his ear about an inch.

"Okay, okay. We just have to stay out of this. Unless, of course, you want to compensate me further."

More shouting.

"Look, let me just lay it on the line here, Jack. You pay me more, or I tell Ollie everything I know, and that's a damn lot at this point."

Krall bit his fingernail as more shouting issued from the receiver. "Time's about up. Pilate is out there in the snow with the evidence right now. I can either help him get the evidence out of town to indict your pal Ollie, or I can help Ollie eliminate Pilate and make sure the blood splatters all over you. The choice is yours, and my suggestion is that you get out your checkbook."

Krall grimaced as a torrent of coarse cursing collided with his eardrums.

"No, *fuck you*. Feel better?"

Jack Lindstrom responded in a normal tone of voice.

"Much better. So we're agreed on $20K? I make sure Pilate gets that evidence to the state police before Ollie catches up to him, right?"

Lindstrom grudgingly agreed, insulted Krall's maternal parentage, and slammed the receiver down.

Krall pushed the flash button for a new dial tone.

"Ollie? It's Krall. Yep, I just found out. Lindstrom admitted it. He bankrolled this Pilate queer to dig up dirt on you. Lindstrom's staying here. He ordered Pilate to get out of town tonight and get to the state police."

He listened for a moment.

"What? No. I doubt he'll go home. He'll probably try to find a four-wheel drive."

More listening, and Krall's eyes were pointed toward the fireplace, though he wasn't really paying the flames any attention.

"You want me to what? Hey, that's not the deal. I'm strictly intelligence. I don't do field work."

He listened to Ollie forming deliberate words around a cigar stub clenched in his teeth.

"Well, when you put it that way…okay. I'll find him and let Craig and Steve know, but I'm tellin' ya right now I ain't gonna have no part in the nasty bit."

Krall placed the phone back in its cradle. He drained the mug, refilled it, and drained it again. He pitched the Cross yearbook in the fire and watched young Ollie Olafson's face burn away as he reached for the scotch bottle one more time.

Krall's right about one thing, Pilate thought. *I'm in a bad spot.* He knew he had very few options, and far too many of them would set off a chain of events that would get him in big trouble at best or killed at worst. *And Kate will likely resent me for doing harm to her child's family name.* "Damn it," he said aloud. *The only safe thing I can do is pack up my car and leave right now. I'll have to just dump the ledger and the letter in the mail to the FBI and go.* Of course, it would have made matters easier if his car weren't still being held hostage in Jimmy's shop.

As he rounded the block leading to his street, he saw the sheriff's truck parked in front of his apartment.

"Crap." His stomach rolled again.

Pilate ducked down an alley between two houses, his breath issuing visibly as he panted. He didn't know what the sheriff wanted, but now was definitely not the time to find out.

He crept through the alley, heading toward Kate's. It was at least a fifteen-minute walk, especially if he was trying to be stealthy.

Except for upsetting a few dogs that were unlucky enough to live outside during the harsh winter, Pilate made it to the back alley behind Kate's house. Lights were on in her upstairs window and in the kitchen.

He found a good vantage point and saw Deputy Lenny in his truck, watching the house from the street. The bearded deputy was smoking a cigar and drinking from a thermos.

Pilate figured he could creep up behind the house without Lenny noticing. As quickly and quietly as he could, Pilate ran from tree to tree, hiding for a moment at each tree until he reached the back door. He tested the door, and of course, Kate had locked it. All things considered, he couldn't blame her.

My kingdom for a town with cell service.

He glanced upward and saw the upstairs light go out. A moment later, Kate's shadow moved in the kitchen. He searched for something he might be able to use to throw at the window to get her attention, but the snow covered his options completely. He decided he'd just have to risk knocking on the back door and hope Kate didn't alert the deputy.

He walked up the back steps and knocked twice. Through the sheer curtains over the glass window in the door, he saw Kate stop, look sharply at the door, and then rush to the cabinet.

Her gun! Shit! "Kate," he said, sotto vocce. "It's me, John. Please let me in. It's okay."

Kate cautiously moved closer to the door. He heard her tell Kara to go to the living room and wait by the front door. She approached the door and extended her pistol-filled hand to part the curtains.

Pilate turned on his flashlight and shone it under his chin.

Kate jumped back a step, then sighed and rolled her eyes. She unlocked, unchained, and opened the door. "John, you scared the crap out of me," she said.

"Sorry," he said, stepping into the warm kitchen, the smell of pot roast and potatoes making him hungry again.

"Mommy? Is it okay?" Kara called from the living room.

"Yes, sweetie. It's just Mr. Pilate, coming for dinner."

Kate put the pistol back in a drawer of the cabinet.

"I don't mean to intrude," he said.

Kara walked in. "Hi," she said, hurrying up to hug her mother's leg.

"Hello, Kara," Pilate said, standing there in his dirty coat, his hair mussed from his travels.

"Mr. Pilate is going to eat dinner with us, so please sit down, and I'll get him a plate."

Kara obeyed her mother, who nodded at Pilate.

He took off his coat and draped it over the back of the chair and sat. It felt good to get off his feet.

Kate placed a plate, knife, fork, and spoon in front of him, along with a glass of milk.

"Thanks," he said, smiling cheerily at Kara.

"You look tired and messy," Kara declared.

"Kara Jane!" Kate said, almost laughing.

"Yes, I suppose I do, Kara."

Kate placed the pot roast, mashed potatoes, and carrots on the table. "Kara, will you thank God for our food, please?" Kate said, placing her napkin in her lap.

Kara bent her head and clasped her hands in prayer, and Kate and Pilate followed her lead.

"God bless this food. Thank you for the snow and please take care of Grandpa and Mommy and our friend the pilot because Mama thinks he's cute. Amen."

"Thank you, dear," Kate said, blushing.

Pilate smiled; he saw much of Kate in Kara's eyes.

Kate put small amounts of meat and vegetables on Kara's plate, and the little girl made a face at the carrots. "You just thanked God for those carrots. Don't wrinkle your nose at them."

"Okay," she said in mock exasperation. She ate a carrot, then attacked her mashed potatoes.

"You want gravy?" Kate asked.

Kara shook her head.

"John, please eat." She passed him the potatoes and other entrees one at a time, serving herself after Pilate.

Pilate ate a bite of the most tender roast he had tasted since the last time he'd had his grandmother's Sunday dinner. Contrary to what Dinty Moore was serving up, hers was obviously real beef. "Oh my g...goodness," Pilate said. "This is excellent."

Kate smiled. "Thanks. We try to have a nice Sunday dinner."

"Mommy made Jell-O too!" Kara announced.

"Yes, but you only get some if you clean your plate," she said.

Kara nodded, hesitantly shoveling roast in her tiny mouth. "Chew, young lady," Kate scolded. Then she turned to her uninvited guest. "So, John, what's going on?"

"Well," he said, reluctantly putting down his fork. "I ran across some interesting things when I went sightseeing today."

Kate's features darkened. "Oh?"

"Any word on Grif?" he said.

"No change," she said. "What did you see?"

"Something that some people might go to great lengths to acquire."

Kate looked puzzled.

"Why not let me show you after dinner?"

Kate nodded and reminded Kara to wipe her chin.

After dinner, Kara took her Jell-O into the living room to watch a Disney video. Kate made coffee, and Pilate filled her in on the events of the day.

"Damn it, John. I can't believe you did that," she said. Her eyes flashed anger and hurt. "I could have let you in the mortuary. Why didn't you tell me about your suspicions?"

"Because you're being watched by the sheriff, and I also didn't want you put in any danger."

"So that's why you show up at my back door after dark, under the very nose of the sheriff? Nice logic." She threw her cloth napkin on the table.

"Kate, you can be pissed at me all you want, but I think you need to know what I found," he said. He reached behind him and pulled the ledger out of his pocket and laid it on the table.

She eyed it for a moment. "What is it?"

He removed the letter from the book, unfolded it carefully, and handed it to her.

"It looks a little, uh, burnt." She sniffed it. "And recently." "Yeah. Krall threw it in the fireplace," Pilate said.

"What? Krall? Why the hell did Krall have it? I thought you found it," she said.

"I did," he said. "I showed it to Krall because I thought he might know what to do next," he said.

"Brilliant move, Einstein. Krall's a nut," she said.

"Maybe, but he's a nut who wants me to destroy this and leave town," he said. "Just read it."

Pilate watched Kate's face change as she read the letter.

"Sweet Jesus," she said. "This was in Brady Bernard's ashes? In Grif's mortuary? I thought those ashes were destroyed in that fire years ago."

"Well, they weren't...and somebody wants this letter very badly," Pilate said.

"Who? Olafson? How would he even know it existed?"

"Krall and I think Jack Lindstrom started spreading rumors to discredit Olafson," Pilate said. "Or maybe even to get him in trouble with the law so Jack could get the land he wants."

"But how could Lindstrom know there was a letter?" Kate's face was screwed up in confusion.

"I think he just knew about the town history, and he heard the rumors and figured he would just start a little trouble for Ollie. It was Lindstrom's way of playing hardball. I'm sure the arrogant ass had no idea that he was actually exposing something that really happened."

"Grif said Jack was hassling him the other night before we came over." Her eyes looked faraway as she recalled the conversation. "All he would say is that Jack was trying to dig up some dirt on Ollie."

"Makes sense," Pilate said.

"All those years ago they murdered a kid and dropped him in the river," Kate said. "Why?"

"Not sure. I guess he got crossways with the car theft ring somehow."

"And Brady Bernard was just a coincidence?"

"Well, he knew about it, that's for sure. I think they also killed Martin Nathaniel way back when. I think Martin knew about the murder of the black kid, and they were sending a message to Martin, Grif, and anybody else who was involved to keep their mouth shut," he said. "Hey, do you care if I smoke?"

She pointed to the back door. "Sure. Why not ask Deputy Lenny for a light?"

He sighed.

"So you think Martin was in on the car ring and got nervous when they killed the kid? You think Ollie and his dad decided he was a risk?"

Pilate nodded. "I think they ran him off the bridge. They're pretty good at that sort of thing, from what I understand. I doubt they were trying to kill Martin, especially considering they thought he probably knew the whereabouts of the ledger. I'm sure they just wanted to scare him."

"So they've kept an eye out for the ledger all these years. They figure Grif doesn't have a clue about it. It gets whispered about for forty-plus years, then Dandy Jack starts spreading rumors that something has been found that will ruin the Olafsons," she said. "So Ollie panics and breaks into the crypt looking for it."

"Elementary, my dear Watson. Then when he finds nothing there, he decides to go beat it out of Grif, who probably has no idea where it is," Pilate said.

"But all this means that Kara's grandfather and great-grandfather were accessories to murder," she said, her voice barely above a whisper.

"I'm afraid so, Kate." He looked at the ledger on the tabletop. "And now you, me, and Krall know about it," she said. "Krall won't tell anybody, I'm sure of it," Pilate said.

"John, who do you think filled Lindstrom in on the whole Bernard murder? Who is the guy with all the facts, files, and rumor control in Cross?"

Pilate felt nauseated. "Oh God. What have I done?"

"You trusted the wrong person," she said, looking away. She stood and retrieved her pistol. "And we also have no idea whether the sheriff will help us or not. His family is implicated in that letter. Do you have a gun?"

"Nope." He held up his hands in mock surrender.

"Pacifist." "I have a small pistol in the drawer of my nightstand," she said.

"Leave it there," he said. "I just think we need to gather everybody up and get out of town, head for Goss City and the local P.D. Surely they can help us."

"Not a bad idea," she said, "except for three things. One, the deputy is out front watching my house and car. Two, the roads are nearly impassable as it is. And three, I think it's getting worse." She opened the curtains on the back door, exposing massive snowflakes falling to the ground, piling up in three-foot drifts.

"So we call the state patrol?" Pilate said. "Now?"

"Yes, we should," Kate said. She located her phone directory, found the number, and picked up the phone. She dialed, then held the phone from her ear a second; she pressed the on and off button a few times. "Dead," she said.

"Um, I think I'd like to change my stance on gun control," Pilate said.

"We need to get somewhere safe," Pilate said. "Ya think?" she said.

"You're just great at concealing your sarcasm," Pilate said. He took her hand in his. "Listen, there has to be someone in this town we can trust, preferably within walking distance."

"John, my house is at the end of the street. You had to cross through several alleys and a couple of fields to get here," she said. "If Lenny weren't such a shitty cop, you would've been caught. By now I'm sure they're actively looking for you. It's only a matter of time before they come knocking on my door."

"That's why we have to get out of here," he said. "Look, we can sneak out the back. The snow is coming down so hard that there's no way Lenny'll see us. We could head to a friendly place."

"I can't think of too many people in this town who'd hide us. They're all too scared of Ollie and the sheriff," she said.

"Damn it."

"I know somebody." He stood up. "Get Kara into her snowsuit. You bundle up, too, and while you're upstairs, get me that other gun."

CHAPTER SEVENTEEN

Kara sat in the kitchen, her pink Barbie snowsuit covering nearly every inch of her, while her mother gathered some things from upstairs. "Why are we going for a walk so late?" Kara asked Pilate.

"Pretty snow out there," he said. "It'll be fun."

"It's cold...and dark," she said.

"Your mommy and I will be with you," Pilate said.

"I'm not going," Kara said, folding her arms across her chest, mittens hanging from her sleeves.

"What if..." Pilate reached in his pocket. "What if I could make this quarter disappear? Then would you go?"

She looked at him quizzically, then nodded.

Pilate produced the quarter, showed it to her, and then did some razzmatazz hand gestures. He finished with both hands open and empty.

"Where did it go?" Kara said, her eyes wide.

"Magic. So now will you go?"

"Bring it back."

"If I do, then you'll come with us, right?"

"Okay."

More razzmatazz. He reached toward Kara, but instead of pulling the quarter from her ear as he had done to his nieces hundreds of time before, he pulled away from her, this time with no quarter.

"It's gone!" she said with a gasp.

"Really? Are you sure? Why don't you put on your mittens," he said, smiling.

She slowly complied. Her face broke into a wide smile as she pulled the quarter from her mitten. "Do it again!"

"After we get done with our walk," he said.

Kate came downstairs, pulling on her coat. "I'm ready, John."

"Are the lights on a timer?" he asked.

"Yes, I set them to go on and off at intervals for the next few hours," she said. "If they decide to keep watching the house, they'll assume I'm here."

"All right," he said, checking the view from the curtains of the back window.

"Mommy, Mr. Pilate is magic," Kara said, still delighted.

"Yes he is, Kara—in more ways than one."

Pilate smiled, hoping not to betray to Kate his anxiety and fear.

The trio crept out the back door and into the snowy night. Kate and Pilate agreed that heading straight through the three-acre soybean field directly to a row of old houses on Jefferson Street was the most direct route.

Pilate carried Kara piggyback, with Kate running alongside as they trudged through the blinding snow and rutted ground.

"This is fun!" Kara squealed.

"Glad you think so," Pilate said over his shoulder with a grunt.

"Kara be quiet," Kate said.

"We're almost there," John panted. In the midst of all that moisture, his throat was dry.

"John, what if he's not home?" Kate said.

"On a night like this?"

"Good point," she said.

Within about twenty minutes of stumbling through the snowy fields, they reached their destination.

John looked around the neighborhood. It was quiet except for sound of the snow crunching under their feet. He put Kara down on the porch. She went to Kate and stood next to her. John knocked at the door.

In a moment, the door opened.

"Jesus, Pilate! You picked a helluva time to visit," Trevathan said.

Sitting around Trevathan's fireplace sipping hot chocolate, Pilate was wary of explaining everything to the Dean, but Trevathan was his last hope for refuge.

"We would have called first, but our phone was out," Kate said.

"Humph," Trevathan said, reaching for his own phone. He tapped the receiver a few times. "Mine's out too. Ice must've knocked over a tree on the phone lines or something. Happens."

The ever-familiar stomach lurch hit Pilate again.

Trevathan's glass eye wandered a little as he faced Kara and Kate. "Do you want marshmallows in that, sweetie?"

Kara shook her head slowly; the glass eye was creeping her out, Pilate supposed.

"No thanks," Kate said. "We appreciate you letting us in, Dr. Trevathan."

"Yes," Pilate said. "Sir, I wouldn't mind marshmallows. Could you show me where they are?"

Trevathan looked bemused, then said "Oh, of course." The pair excused themselves and went into the kitchen.

"Jee-sus, Mr. Pilate, trouble follows you everywhere you go," he said, leaning against the cabinet, folding his arms over his flannel shirt.

"I know," Pilate said. "It's a gift."

"You know you're fired? Lindstrom demanded I let your contract go at the end of semester. Seems he heard about your little accident on the road the other day."

"Yeah." Pilate nodded. "What's the official reason going to be for my termination?"

Trevathan hocked something in his throat. "Shit if I know. Probably say we don't need a speech teacher or your beard tickled when you kissed his ass."

"Well, that's the least of my problems." Pilate rubbed his hands together to thaw them. "Look, I don't want to implicate you in any of this, and I'm sure I already have by coming here, but I really think our lives are in danger."

"Goddamn right your lives are in danger," Trevathan said, peering out the window. "From what I can see, you've managed to get in between a pissing match of epic proportions. Ollie stands to make millions on this land deal, but that's gonna be tough to do from behind bars. There's no statute of limitations on murder. If he's out of the picture, Jackass Lindstrom gets the land to expand the school. I just wanna know what you found out that's so important that it's got them after you like this."

Pilate removed the ledger from his pocket and placed it on the kitchen table.

Trevathan picked it up and thumbed through it, hovering on a couple of pages before he handed it back to Pilate. "A ledger? Doesn't look all that damning to me. Those initials could be anybody's."

"True, but I also found this." Pilate carefully unfolded the letter.

As Trevathan read, his glass eye danced in its socket. Without looking away from the letter, he pulled a chair out from the table and sat down. "Jee-sus."

Pilate sat opposite him, the gun in his pocket weighing heavily.

"Brady Bernard," Trevathan rasped. "Brady fucking Bernard? He knew everything. This is the goddamned Rosetta stone, John. Where'd you find it?"

Pilate told him of finding the ledger and letter amidst the mortal remains of the most notorious professor in Cross College history.

"In his ashes? Aw, you gotta be shittin' me." He paused, snapped his fingers, and looked up.

"That was why they broke into the crypts. They got an idea that there was some evidence floating around." He was quiet a moment, then grinned. "Wait a minute! So this is all just a big coincidence? Bernard murdered the president back then for totally different reasons, but he became a part of this when Martin Nathaniel dumped the evidence in his ashes for safekeeping? Fantastic story."

"I think Martin meant to retrieve the book from the ashes before they could be claimed, but they ran him off the road and killed him, and nobody had any idea where the book and letter were," Pilate said. "Ollie Sr. probably assumed they'd been lost or destroyed. Grif probably shoved the ashes in the closet when he took over the company after Martin was killed."

"Grif got his ass beat for this, yet he knows nothing?" Trevathan said, holding the letter up to the light.

"I think so. I mean, I think Grif was aware of what was happening with the car theft ring, and maybe the murder of that kid scared him. After Martin died, he probably figured it was in his best interests to keep his mouth shut and forget about the whole thing."

"Imagine if Brady Bernard had anybody in his life who loved him," Trevathan said softly. "Somebody would have claimed the ashes and blown this whole thing wide open years ago."

"But they didn't, yet somehow I did," Pilate said.

Trevathan took a minute to digest what he'd just learned.

"Krall thinks Lindstrom made up the whole thing to panic Ollie," Pilate said. "What the sick fuck didn't count on was that it might actually be true."

"Wait…Derek Krall knows about this? You told him?" Trevathan said.

"I know, I know. Dumb move." Pilate looked down in shame. "I-I thought I could trust him."

"He's on Lindstrom's payroll, John." Trevathan looked disgusted.

"Well, so are we, in a manner of speaking," Pilate said.

"No, John. What I mean is, Krall's the one who's researched all this town history shit for Lindstrom. Can't you see? He fed it to you so you'd dig into it. You've been set up, my naïve friend."

Pilate limped over to the sink, feeling like he was going to throw up yet again. He turned on the water and heaved, but nothing came. He reached for the tap to run some cold water to splash his face and caught the image of Simon reflected in the small kitchen window above the sink. "Christ!"

"John? You okay?" Trevathan said, rising to his feet.

Pilate breathed heavily. "Yeah."

"I'm sorry I didn't warn you more carefully. I only figured out Krall's role in all this just now, but all the pieces fit. Did Krall give you information about the Bernard murder thing, or did Kate?"

"Krall."

"Of course. He probably had his suspicions. He knew you and Kate have been getting friendly. Never trust a librarian," Trevathan said. "He really played you."

"True," Pilate said, "but this isn't over yet. I need to get out of here." He looked into Trevathan's good eye. "Is it unmanly to say I'm scared to death?"

"Nope. You'd be an idiot not to be," Trevathan said. "I'd tell you to take my truck and get to the city right now, but there is no way in hell you're gonna be able to get out of town. But, John, you can't stay here."

Pilate felt like he'd been kicked in the gut.

"Don't take it personally, my friend, but you have to get away from Kate and that little angel of hers. If they show up here looking for you, I think I can protect them. They have roots in this town, and Ollie's bunch knows damn well I'm armed to the teeth. But if you're here…well, I don't know what would happen."

"What do I do?"

"You armed?"

Pilate pulled Kate's pistol out of his pocket.

"What is that, a twenty-five Mauser? That's a pea shooter." He snorted and waved the weapon away as if it was nothing more than a squirt gun. "Be right back."

Pilate felt a passing twinge of suspicion that he shouldn't let the geezer out of his sight, but he was just too tired and too resigned to distrust him. Besides that, he knew he really had no choice.

Trevathan turned on the TV for Kara. He paused a moment and straightened a framed photo on the mantle of someone Kate presumed was his deceased wife, then climbed the stairs.

Kate came in the kitchen and stood beside the table.

"We can trust him," Pilate said.

"You saying that for my benefit or your own?" she said.

"Ha. Listen, Kate, I think you two should stay here, but I should find somewhere else to hide out," he said.

"And where the hell will you go? It's freezing out there, John. The snow is at least three feet deep already and shows no sign of stopping." Kate pulled Trevathan's chair up to Pilate and sat beside him, looking him in the eyes. "You're not exactly James Bond, you know. You won't make it out there."

"Thanks for the vote of confidence," he said, trying to be light. "I'll be okay."

Trevathan walked in carrying two handguns. He handed one to Pilate. "This black one's a Glock nine. It has a kick, but it holds seventeen shots." Holding up a nickel-plated revolver, he said, "This is a Smith and Wesson. It's a wheel gun, only holds six shots, but you don't risk a jam. Your choice."

Kate blanched. "Oh God. You really think this could end badly, don't you?"

Trevathan could only offer a pained smile. "Miss Nathaniel, I like to plan for the worst and feel silly later rather than end up dead of embarrassment. Better tried by twelve than carried by six."

"You sure this Mauser won't be sufficient?"

Trevathan turned it over in his hands, examining the action and the cartridges. "This thing hasn't been cleaned in years…and it's old." He pointed at his glass eye. "Dirty old guns are as bad as dirty old men. How do you think I lost my eye?"

Pilate removed the clip from the Glock, reinserted it, and set the safety, just as his grandfather had taught him so many summers ago with a World War II-issue forty-five. "This will do. That other one's a little too Dirty Harry for me," Pilate said. "This one is more James Bond." He winked at Kate.

"Suit yourself," Trevathan said. "I expect you to give that back to me personally."

"Where's he going to go? We can't just send him out there into that mess alone," Kate said, her eyes brimming with angry tears.

Trevathan pulled a heavy ring of keys from a fish-shaped key minder hanging on his wall. "I know a place."

CHAPTER EIGHTEEN

The snow continued to fall for another hour while Trevathan drew a map of the safest route for Pilate to get to his destination. It led back to the Cross College campus, through a back door of the library, and into the clock tower. "Here's the security code for the door. Once you unlock it, you have about ten seconds to punch in this code, or the alarm will go off. Of course, if phone lines are down, the security system may not even work.
Just assume it does to be safe."

"Okay," Pilate said. "I would be shocked if anyone suspects me of holing up there." He put his arm around Kate. "I can do this, Kate."

"I know," she said, her arm slipping around his waist.

"Okay. Enough of that," Trevathan said. "Get to the tower. Here's the key to the room that houses the bells and carillon system. It's warm in there, and you'll have a view of most of the campus. Get in there and stay put until morning, then I'll get word to the state patrol about what's going on."

"I can't just sit up there, can I?" Pilate said.

"Well, what else do you suggest?"

"At daybreak, I can head for the highway," he said.

"Pretty dangerous. Scovill's truck can maneuver pretty well, even in this muck," Trevathan said, rubbing his cheek.

"What are you hoping for? That a trooper will happen along and pick you up?"

"No. I was thinking I could hike back to Nathaniel's and use his police radio."

"John, just let me handle this," he said.

"Grif does have a police radio. They use it for civil defense since his place is also a backup morgue," Kate offered, regretting the mention of the morgue.

"There's no way the roads here in town are going to be dug out by tomorrow. I can't wait, and they could hurt you guys trying to find me. I'll get out of here, wait in the bell tower until the snow lets up or just before daybreak, whatever comes first. Just let me do this."

Trevathan looked at Kate, then Pilate. "I can't fault your logic. That's the best plan. Let me get you some more seasonable clothes. I have hunting socks, cold-weather pants, thermal underwear, and a heavier winter coat for you."

Pilate changed into the dean's hunting clothes, which were tight on him and would probably hinder him if he tried to run; albeit the snow and his bruised knee and ankle had already effectively crippled that method of escape—at least for the night anyway. He accepted two extra clips of ammunition, some chemical hand warmer packets, and a couple of energy bars. Trevathan also filled a small canteen with water for him. Then, Pilate made the mistake of slipping the smaller pistol in his belt and placing the Glock in his right coat pocket.

"Don't do that," Trevathan said. "Amateur! Here." He handed Pilate a shoulder holster. "Keeps it out of the way and doesn't advertise."

"Thanks," Pilate said. "I really appreciate all this."

"Think nothing of it. I'm ready to retire from this shithole anyway."

"Oh?"

"I have a place in Key West," he said, forcing a smile. "Not too far from Sloppy Joe's. Figure someday I'll write a book about Hemingway and his multi-toed cats."

Pilate turned to Kate, who stood in the living room watching Kara sleep on the couch, her arms folded tightly across her chest. "I'll be back…with help," Pilate said.

"I know. Just be careful, John. These people are crazy." Tears rolled freely down her face. "John, do you think they killed Rick too?" The question startled Pilate. In the excitement, he hadn't considered the death of her husband. "I don't think so. Why would they?"

"Because…" she said, wiping her eyes and nose with a tissue. "Because he started asking a lot of questions after the fire at the mortuary. He started saying he thought it was arson. Rick even made some calls to the state police and the FBI."

"When did he have his wreck?"

"A few months after the fire," she said, hugging Pilate close.

"Oh God, Kate," he said. "I just don't know, but we're going to blow this thing wide open. I promise."

"I don't want them to hurt Kara or Grif or you," she said, sobbing.

Pilate squeezed her tight for a moment. He took her by the shoulders. "Kate, look at me."

She looked into his eyes.

"This killing, all this bad stuff, it's going to end now," he said. "No one else is going to get hurt."

"John, you better get moving," Trevathan said, his voice low.

"Okay," he said. Pilate kissed Kate, then the top of Kara's head, and walked over to Trevathan, extending a hand.

"Thanks, boss. Take care of them."

"Just a concerned old codger," he said, shaking Pilate's hand. "I'll see you soon."

Pilate nodded and stepped toward the kitchen back door. He switched off the light in the kitchen.

"Get ready," Trevathan said. "And John…"

"Yes?"

He heard the cocking of the Smith and Wesson in the dark. "Nobody's going to get in here."

Pilate ducked outside into the deluge, moving as quickly as he could into the first leg of his mile-long trek through the blizzard to the Cross College library.

The maze of alleys, backstreets, and trails Trevathan had shown him were fraught with numerous hazards, including snow-covered potholes, trashcans, and patches of invisible ice. He fell twice, the shock to his bruised knee thankfully absorbed by Trevathan's padded snow gear. It was two in the morning, and visibility was nearly zero.

After forty-five minutes, Pilate crept up to the back of the library. The door was made of rusting old metal, set next to a loading dock. The sodium light above the door was partially obscured by ice. *So far, so good.*

He removed his gloves and fished in his pocket for the key. He found it and pushed it into the lock, but it wouldn't fit. Assuming he was using the wrong one, he tried the other key, but it was a no go as well.

Pilate used his mini-flashlight to check the keys again. *Nope. These are the right keys.* Both had small tags on them: One said *"library,"* and the other said *"bells."* He shone the light on the lock and saw that it was frozen.

"Shit."

He ducked into a small alcove under the loading dock to consider his options. He could try and make it to the mortuary in the storm and risk getting lost and freezing to death, but that wasn't the most favorable idea. He would have to try to warm the lock somehow. He mentally inventoried the contents of his pockets. He didn't have any deicer, and his lighter wouldn't stay lit in the wind. What he did have, however, were the small packets hunters carried in their gloves to keep their hands warm. Pilate removed two of the packets, activated them, and pressed them against the lock. He knew it would take a while, giving him time to be pelted with more ice and snow.

"Well, aren't you the regular action movie star?" Simon said.

"Hey, pal," Pilate said.

"You're going to get yourself killed, you know."

"Well, then, Simon, you die with me, don't you?" Pilate pressed harder against the lock.

"That's a good point, John. Work harder, you piece of shit."

He tried the lock a few times over the next ten minutes. He felt the key going in further each time. Pilate just had to hope it worked before someone drove by in a snow plow or a snow- equipped police vehicle.

Ten more minutes passed, and Pilate was wearing out. He shoved the key in once more. This time it went in all the way. He turned the lock, and the heavy metal door creaked open, displacing powdery snow from the threshold.

His ears were assaulted by the beeping of the security system. "Nice to know something works," he said. He found the glowing digital pad for the system and entered the numbers with his gloved hand. He fat-fingered it and the screen read *"Armed: not accepted."*

"Damn it," he said, biting the fingers of his glove and jerking it off his hand. He punched the numbers and hit the enter button. The beeping stopped, and the screen read *"Disarmed: accepted."*

Standing in the darkness beside the library study carrels, Pilate shivered from a combination of cold, adrenaline, and pure nerves. He quietly stamped snow from his boots and brushed it off his lower pant legs.

He padded through the empty library, using only his wits and sense of touch to find the stairwell to the tower. He climbed one flight and came to the second floor entry.

Seized with an idea, he opened the door and felt around until he came across a photocopier. He hit the on switch and waited for it to warm up.

After he finished with the photocopier, he climbed to the top level of the clock tower and used Trevathan's key to open the door to the carillon room. Inside the room, he found a small stool and a device that looked like a stereo deck from the 1970s, the electronic carillon. Red lights danced on its face next to indicators that read "*standby*." The carillon was mercifully turned off after eleven most nights so the town could sleep in peace. It was set to come back on at seven a.m.

Colored glass windows, about a foot wide and three feet tall, were on each of the four walls. From outside the clock tower, they appeared pretty, but from inside, they obscured his view.

Pilate surmised the actual bells were just above him. Shining his flashlight up quickly, he saw a trapdoor in the ceiling, about ten feet high. Quasimodo he was not.

He sat back a moment, lit a cigarette, and contemplated how he had come hundreds of miles from a broken life and fallen right into the middle of a small town murder drama. He thought of his parents and how it would crush them if he died alone in that abysmal town. *They'll probably find my body in my car, crashed in a ditch—or maybe I'll join that poor black kid at the bottom of the Missouri, chained to my steering column, my lips gone and my skull eternally smiling.*

"*Cheery,*" Simon said.

"Yeah, it is."

"*It's not over yet, you know.*"

"I know." Pilate exhaled. "How come I'm smoking this time? It's usually you."

"*Go figure. Perhaps I've had enough of living dangerously.*"

"Amen, brother."

"*Smart move, by the way, John.*"

"What?"

"*Photocopying the Bernard letter,*" he said. "*And how dramatic, putting copies of it in those books in particular.*" Simon's laugh rattled around Pilate's head.

Pilate smiled at his own cleverness. He'd tucked a copy of the Bernard letter into the *Book of John* in the large century-old Bible on display in the philosophy section. He'd also put a copy in Leslie Charteris's *The Saint*. "I couldn't resist."

"You better take a nap. You should rest for a while and check the snow again around four," Simon sounded kindly in Pilate's head. His trademark sharp, sarcastic tone was gone.

"Who are you, my mother?"

"Simon says."

Pilate crushed out the cigarette with the heel of his boot, drew his coat around him, and quickly dozed off.

When the bells chimed four times, he sat straight up, screaming, "What? Huh?" When he regained his wits by the fourth chime, he realized that though the carillon was not playing show tunes, the bells would still chime on the hour.

"Have we heard the chimes at midnight?" Simon said.

His chest thumping, he took deep breaths to calm himself. He stood and peered out the yellow stained glass window facing east. The snow was lighter now; he could see it falling in smaller flakes against the antique globes of the lamps of the quad below.

Now or never, he thought. He zipped his coat, slipped on his gloves, and opened the door. He locked it behind him and crept back down to the study carrels by the back door, then reached for the keypad of the security system.

"Hello, John Pilate," Derek Krall's voice erupted from the darkness.

PILATE'S CROSS

CHAPTER NINETEEN

"Krall, get out of my way," Pilate said, his eyes just making out Krall's shape in front of him.

"Now, John, don't do anything stupid. I'm here to help you," he said.

"Help me?" Pilate felt the Glock in the holster under his arm.

"Yes." Krall's voice was calm.

"What are you going to do, set me up again? You've done a fairly masterful job of sticking my ass in the middle of all this, of making me the fall guy."

"Well, what can I say? You were in the right place at the right time. You were so obvious. What you didn't tell me, I easily tracked as you surfed the Internet doing your research. You really are way too trusting, John."

Wait…Krall did give me the free wireless hookup and access to the library's LexisNexis subscription. Of course! That bastard tracked everything I've looked up on the Internet! Shit. Now I feel really stupid, Pilate thought, mentally kicking himself.

"John, what's done is done. Just give me the ledger and that letter, and I'll tell everyone involved that you got away. You'll be safe. With no evidence, nobody will believe you. You'll just be another disgruntled employee."

"Oh, I see. Like Brady Bernard?"

"I tried to save you earlier by throwing it all in the fireplace, but you insisted on toying with your fate."

"I can't believe Lindstrom is doing this," Pilate said. "I mean, he's a first-class asshole, sure, but not a damn killer."

"True," Krall said, his shape more visible.

"What's in it for you, though, Krall?"

"John, it's so simple. I work for Lindstrom, yes. The man is a swine, and he did pay me to dig into Ollie's background. What he didn't count on was Ollie paying me three times as much to engineer this little conspiracy."

"Son of a bitch," Pilate said in disbelief. "He owns you."

"Didn't somebody once say that if you appease a man's conscience, you can take his freedom away from him? Besides, Lindstrom's going to have a little accident of his own," Krall said. "Maybe not now, but soon—after things quiet down a little, after you disappear."

"Just admit it, Krall. You won't let me escape if I give you the evidence. You plan to kill me."

"No, I actually don't, but Ollie's son will when he gets here. I'm just going to hold you here until then. Sorry, pal. There's no other way out but through me."

Pilate slowly put his hand in his coat and grasped the Glock grip in the shoulder holster. "Krall, I'm bigger and younger than you, and I have nothing to lose. I'll kick your ass," Pilate said.

"Well, yeah...you probably would if I didn't have this gun." Krall flipped a switch. A lamp on one of the study carrels flicked on.

Pilate's eyes contracted painfully; he crouched down behind a bookshelf for cover.

"Irony of ironies...this gun," Krall said, laughing. "It's a German Luger. Belonged to a fella named Bernard. You may recall he used it a few times, to great effect."

"Where'd you get it?" Pilate called over the shelf.

"Scovill sold it to me in a sheriff's auction," Krall said. "His daddy had saved it for years. Morgan didn't have the heart to keep it lying around. He's too soft, nothing like his daddy. Now that man could get things done—a real Martin

Bormann type. Come down here. Don't make me prove my marksmanship on you."

"I'll just wait here," Pilate said. "Maybe I'll do a little light reading." He pulled the Glock from the holster and quietly loosed the safety. There was already a bullet in the pipe; all he had to do was aim it right.

"John, we can do this easy, or we can do this hard." Krall cleared his throat in his nervous way. "I assure you—you'd rather go easy."

"Can't we make a deal?"

"Sorry, friend, but you don't have a damn thing I want, except maybe that piece of ass, Kate. Of course, since you probably blabbed about all this to her, she won't be around much longer either."

Pilate's anger rose, the one emotion that could conquer his anxiety and nerves. "Krall, she has a little girl," Pilate said, peering over the railing at Krall, who was holding the Luger in front of him, his hand shaking.

"Yeah, I know." He sounded genuinely remorseful. "Another orphan in the world. Look, I didn't create this situation," he said, irritated. "Enough of this bullshit. Please come out now."

"Well, I could stay holed up here until classes start today," Pilate said.

"Sorry, John. It's a snow day. Classes are canceled."

Fuck. "Okay. Goddamn it, I'm coming out. I'm too fucking tired to run anymore," Pilate said. He put the Glock in his coat pocket, keeping his finger on the trigger. Rising and walking down the stairs, he held his left hand up.

"Both hands, John," Krall said, gesturing with the Luger menacingly.

When Pilate was in full view, Krall made a surprisingly fluid motion and pointed the pistol at him. "I'm sorry, John." Krall pulled the trigger, but instead of firing at Pilate, the cartridge exploded in the gun chamber, showering Krall with sparks and tiny shrapnel. Krall dropped the traitorous weapon and covered his bloody face with his hands, screaming. "Mother…fucker," he bleated.

Pilate pulled the gun from his pocket, his hand shaking as he pointed it at Krall, who had slipped into unconsciousness. His chest rose with his breaths, though, and his wounds didn't look life threatening, but his face was lacerated badly from his gun's explosion. "Dirty old guns," Pilate said, stepping over Krall. "Serves you right, asshole."

His ears ringing from the echo of the exploded gun, Pilate sprinted to the back of the library, launched himself from the door, and ran for the tree line that demarcated the town of Cross from the college. Adrenaline got him there in only a moment or two, even on a bum knee, a bad ankle, and in the drifting snow. From there, he had the treacherous trek through the fields to the mortuary and the salvation of the radio.

As he ran, he replayed what had happened to Krall, amazed at his luck and relieved that he hadn't had to try to shoot the treacherous bastard.

The snow drifted as high as five feet in places, and Pilate fell flat on his face just yards away from the deer stand he'd encountered the day before. The frozen snow slapped his face hard. It felt almost like a burn.

Sitting up on his knees, the right one throbbing, he brushed the ice and snow from his face and the front of his coat. He had only about another hour before morning was well and truly there to expose him to his pursuers. His legs ached, and his lungs burned. *Damn cigarettes.*

"Get up, John, Simon says," Pilate muttered.

Pilate got to his feet, putting one foot in front of the other, slogging heavily through the thick snow.

CHAPTER TWENTY

Another hour, another mile. The sun was up, the clouds dampening its enthusiasm enough to give him some cover, but he knew it wouldn't last. Thankfully, the hill overlooking Nathaniel Mortuary was only fifty yards or so away. He pushed himself to crown the hill in a matter of minutes.

Prone on the hilltop, he looked down on the mortuary. Seeing no one, he felt better about the whole adventure.

He stumbled down the hillside to the window he had broken out. Scovill had undoubtedly found it, as it had been covered over with cardboard and duct tape. Pilate kicked the cardboard in with one thrust of his trembling left leg and lowered himself inside.

The morning light leaked in through the windows, though most of the room was cloaked in shadow. He unzipped his ruined coat and felt warmer immediately. The heat was on.

Pilate smelled something he hadn't smelled before: tobacco, cigar smoke to be exact. He also noted an unfamiliar smell that he surmised was heating oil; the floor was covered with it.

Pilate drew his gun, turned off the safety, and looked around. The small desk had been rifled again, much more carelessly this time. The door to the storage closet was broken in. The open cylinder of Brady Bernard's ashes lay on the floor, the cremains dumped everywhere.

The bodies of Martin and Millie Nathaniel still lay on the tables, though their sheets had been removed. Someone had used a scalpel to split open the bodies, looking into the desiccated, crumbling husks in apparent hopes of finding the elusive ledger.

Pilate grimaced, marveling at just how sick and desperate the culprits were. His thoughts were interrupted by the sound of heavy creaking from upstairs, heavy footsteps. "Shit," he whispered.

Pilate had to get to the radio, but it was upstairs with the visitor, and he dreaded the thought of another gunfight. He was sure his luck couldn't possibly hold for a second time, and the person or persons upstairs were no doubt much better at that sort of thing than a middle-aged librarian with a dirty old gun.

"Stinkin' thinkin'," Simon said.

Pilate shivered nervously, shook it off, and moved past the mutilated corpses to the stairs.

Slowly, agonizing over every creak of the stairs and every slip his oily boots made, Pilate climbed to the top. He crouched down two steps below and peered under the door. He saw no feet, so whoever was up there was probably in Grif's office.

Pilate pushed the door partially open. He saw nothing but the filing cabinets and coffee maker. As stealthily as his oil-covered climbing boots would allow, Pilate crossed the small room and stood by the door leading to the mortuary's waiting rooms and offices.

He thought of how self-assured and easy the hero types made such a quest look on TV, and he realized there was a reason that was fiction.

Pilate pondered his options: Once he left that room, he could go into the casket showroom, the small chapel, or the big sitting area. If there was somebody in Grif's office, they probably wouldn't see him slip into the casket showroom. Pilate figured he could hide behind one of the casket displays until the opportune moment to make a move.

Pilate thought a second, wondering how he might determine what that opportune moment was. He supposed they would leave Grif's office at one point or another and then he could get to the radio.

He sprung out of the room, sped across the hallway, and ducked into the casket showroom. The lights were off, but a snow-covered skylight above gave some dim light. Pilate went behind a skirted casket with an open, embroidered lid. He didn't pause to read it, but he could have sworn it featured the logo of the Cross College Cougars.

Behind the casket, Pilate caught his breath and shrugged out of Trevathan's coat. He put the two Glock clips in his hip pocket. He sat as still as he could, listening and trying to stop trembling.

Pilate heard very little for at least fifteen minutes. His legs began to spasm with exhaustion, his stomach roiled, and his head pounded. Panic was creeping in again—the overwhelming dread that he was going to die alone and in pain in a mortuary—and the thought assailed his fragile nerves. He knew his nerve would give out before his worn-out body would, and that time was fast approaching. *I'm so...tired.*

Pilate said a silent prayer, grasped the Glock in his trembling right hand, and stood up, peering at the hallway from behind the casket lid. He inched away from the casket toward the door. A foot or so away from the doorway, he heard the unmistakable sound of keys turning in the lock of the glass front door. He ran back behind the casket, crouching with the Glock ready to fire.

Pilate heard the sounds of the outer door opening and closing. "Morgan, what are you doing here? You find that guy and Kate?"

"Ollie, this has to end. It's gotten out of control," Sheriff Scovill said.

"Morgan, you know damn well that if I go down, your daddy's reputation'll be ruined forever…and yours along with it."

"This isn't about Dad. This is about you and me," Scovill said. "It's about you killing that boy all those years ago. It's about what I think you did to Rick Nathaniel just so you could get rich, you bastard."

"Now, Morgan, put that gun away," Ollie said in a soothing tone. "Rick Nathaniel was a pain in the ass, just like his grandfather. If you're arresting me, you're arresting me. I'll go."

Peering around the lid of the casket, Pilate saw Ollie Olafson's son creeping past the casket showroom doorway, shotgun in hand. Five feet more, and he would have a clear shot at the sheriff.

Craig Olafson looked down and saw Pilate's footprints, the oil he had tracked from downstairs a telltale sign of Pilate's hiding place.

Ollie continued to stall Scovill. "Look, I'm going to make at least two million on this deal. Morg, I can cut you in for half a mill."

"Just get on your knees and put your hands on your head," Scovill said. "I've lived with knowing what happened in '63 for a long time. It's time for me and you to face the music. Now get down like I said," Scovill said.

Pilate darted from behind the casket out of the showroom. His oily boots slipped on the linoleum hallway, though, and he fell hard on his shoulder with an "Oomph."

Craig, shocked by the spectacle, wheeled around and pointed the shotgun at Pilate.

"Scovill!" Pilate rolled up on his good left knee and pointed the Glock at Craig.

Craig fired at Pilate.

Knocked back like a linebacker had hit him, Pilate felt dozens of tiny stings in his left arm, chest, and face. He squeezed the Glock trigger instinctively, but the hapless bullet disappeared into the ceiling.

"Freeze, you son of a bitch!" Scovill said as he wheeled and fired. He put a bullet in Craig's fat head; a corona of blood and brain matter sprayed the hallway and Pilate's pants.

Ollie spat a guttural curse at Scovill and pulled a pistol from the back of his waistband. He fired, hitting Scovill in his right side. Scovill's gun flew out of his hand and skittered to the floor, some five feet away.

Scovill crumpled on the spot, grasping his side, a dark stain forming on his coat. He looked surprised, his squinty eye open as wide as Pilate had ever seen it.

Pilate felt stabbing pains all over his shoulder and chest, as if someone was sitting on him. He could barely catch his breath, and he knew he was quickly fading into shock.

"Up!" Simon bellowed in his head.

Pilate's eyelids flickered like a kid fighting to stay awake late on Christmas Eve. Through sheer force of will, he opened them wide and pointed the Glock at Ollie with a shaking left hand.

Ollie stood over Scovill, his eyes wet with tears. "You killed my boy," he whimpered. "Goddamn you."

Scovill was fading, holding his side with one hand, weakly holding another in front of him in a pathetic attempt to ward off Ollie's next bullet. The question was whether he would pass out or be shot first.

Pilate leveled the Glock at Ollie and said weakly, "Stop."

Ollie barely glanced at him. "Fuck you," he said and aimed the gun at Scovill's head.

Pilate squeezed the trigger repeatedly.

The first two shots missed Ollie, who started to run back into Grif's office. The third shot caught the corrupt mayor in the neck. Ollie dropped his gun as both his hands went to his wound. Pilate fired again, hitting Ollie in the groin. The big man gasped, spat up blood, and fell to the floor.

Scovill clicked his shoulder-mounted walkie-talkie and said in a quavering voice: "We've got an 11-99...11-99! Officer down! Officer down! Shots fired, Nathaniel Mortuary, repeat officer down, shots fired...11...goddamn it! Get an ambulance over here now."

Pilate's eyelids fluttered again. The Glock fell from his hand, making a solid *clunk* as it hit the floor. He tried to open his eyes but only managed one last glimpse of the carnage around him before he was swallowed by darkness.

CHAPTER TWENTY-ONE

"Lucky for you it was birdshot in Craig's gun," Dr. Hutton said, standing at the foot of his hospital bed.

"Funny. I don't feel lucky," Pilate croaked.

"You should. Aside from having trouble getting through metal detectors the rest of your life, the birdshot missed your vital parts. The wounds from the birdshot we removed from your face should heal okay," Hutton said, squeezing his foot gently. "Don't worry. You'll still be pretty."

Pilate managed a painful grin.

"You have a couple of visitors," he said as he walked out. Kate and Kara burst into the small hospital room.

Kate took his hand in hers. "John, Doc Hutton says you're going to be all right."

"I know," he said, squeezing her hand.

"Mr. Pilate, I made you a get well card," Kara said, handing him a construction paper and glitter creation adorned with hearts and stars.

"I love it," he said. "Thank you, Kara."

"I made Grandpa one too," she said.

"Good, good."

"He liked it," she said.

"Grif's awake?" Pilate asked Kate.

She nodded. "Yes, and he is talking to the FBI right now.

They have some questions for you too…when you're ready."

"Yup. How's Scovill?"

"Recovering from surgery. They removed the kidney Ollie shot a hole in," Kate said, sitting on the edge of the bed. "He's going to be all right, but he has a lot to answer for."

"I know, but he did the right thing in the end," Pilate said. "That has to count for something."

"Trooper Hulsey said Scovill told him you saved his life, that you…" She paused a moment and turned to look at her daughter. "Kara, would you go tell the nice nurse at the desk outside that Mr. Pilate needs some ice?"

"Okay, Mommy," Kara said, skipping out of the room.

"Scovill said you shot Ollie," she said.

"Is he…?" He couldn't bear to say the word.

"He bled to death from the neck wound before the ambulance could get there," she said. "I can't say I feel sad about that. Did you shoot Krall too?"

"No. He had a crappy old gun, and it blew up in his face." Pilate rubbed his eyes a moment. "I have such a headache. Is Krall okay?"

"No, John. I think after you left him, Craig's friend Steve finished him off."

He let out a low whistle between his teeth.

"They found him with a bullet in his head. They dumped his body in a snow drift behind the library."

"Bastards."

"Trooper Hulsey said they're looking for Steve. They'll find him. He's not all that bright, and usually on the pipe."

They sat still for a moment.

"Trevathan's out in the hall. He wants to say hi," she said. "He stayed up all night with that gun in his lap. Nobody showed up, but he never once let his guard down. As soon as it was light, he got his truck shoveled out and drove us to the mortuary. By then it was crawling with cops. Looks like Ollie and Craig were going to look harder for the ledger, then burn down the mortuary again."

"Kate, I think they may have killed Rick," Pilate said. "I know," she said softly.

"I'm so sorry."

"Thank you, John. You helped bring some justice for Rick," she said. "That means so much to me."

Pilate squeezed her hand again. "Why don't you tell Trevathan to come in?" Pilate said. "I want to thank him."

Trevathan shuffled in the room; he looked exhausted but managed a smile.

"Thanks, Doc," Pilate said.

"No problem," Trevathan said. "Where's my gun?"

"What about Lindstrom?" Pilate said and smiled.

"The FBI has some questions about his involvement in all this, John," he said, sitting in the chair by Pilate's bed. "I'm thinking conspiracy charges at the very least."

"Sounds good to me," Pilate said.

"The news media is crawling all over this. I suspect they'll start looking at his business transactions and other such activities pretty damn closely." Trevathan smiled with what could only be deemed immense satisfaction. "Looks like the Lindstrom Renaissance is over. But shit, this country college was never meant to be Harvard on the Missouri."

"Doc?"

"Yeah?"

"Am I still fired?"

The next morning, Pilate had his hospital breakfast of cardboard scrambled eggs, yogurt, toast, and bad coffee that was in desperate need of sugar. He eased out of the bed, slid into a robe, and went in search of sugar. He waved at the duty nurses. "Can I get some sugar?"

The nurses laughed.

"I meant for my coffee," he said, smiling painfully. The birdshot wounds in his face ached.

The nurses suggested he go down the hall to their break room. Pilate gingerly padded down the hospital hallway, trying to suppress the urge to look into the rooms of other patients as he walked by. He couldn't help himself though. One room was darkened, and there was an empty chair next to a bed with a man on a ventilator. One room was filled with people, crowded around a beloved family member, Pilate guessed.

He was not only happy to be out of his hospital bed, but to be alive at all. Every breath he drew was painful due to his wounds, and his knee and ankle throbbed, but he also felt a strange euphoria. *Must be the pain meds.*

In the nurses' break room, dug through a million pink packets of artificial sweetener, and finally found three packets of the real stuff. He slipped them into the pocket of his robe and left the break room, but instead of going back the way he came, he went down the hall in the other direction.

Sitting outside a patient room was a sloppy man in an ill-fitting uniform, reading a *Cross Courier*.

"Hi," Pilate said.

The deputy lowered the newspaper and looked at Pilate impassively.

"I suppose, uh…that you have orders not to let anyone in there, eh, Lenny?" Pilate said, glancing at the front-page photo of himself being loaded onto an ambulance.

Lenny stood up, looked at the door, then back at Pilate. He made a go-ahead gesture, then opened the door for Pilate.

"Thanks, Lenny. I won't be long."

Pilate went inside and walked up to the bed that contained the soon-to-be-ex-sheriff.

Morgan Scovill was asleep. A monitor beeped softly beside his bed.

Pilate stood there a moment, unsure of what to do. He decided not to disturb Scovill and turned to leave.

"Where you going?" Scovill croaked.

Pilate didn't turn around.

"I was trying to get out of here before you release one of those deadly farts of yours," Pilate said.

"I got so many holes in me I'd probably fart out the wrong place," Scovill said. "Lenny let you in?"

"Yeah, chatty as ever." Pilate walked over beside Scovill. "You okay, Sheriff?"

"I've been better," he rasped. "Can you give me some ice?"

Pilate scooped some ice out of a plastic cup with a special straw and put some on Scovill's lips.

He crunched the ice and swallowed thirstily. "Want more?"

Scovill signaled that he did not.

"Sheriff, I'm sorry all this happened the way it did," Pilate said.

"Don't be. It had to come out eventually," he said. "I'd been turnin' a blind eye to Ollie's shit for way too long. I was covering my dad's ass, but it still wasn't right of me."

Pilate nodded. "Is that why you kept me in the loop? Were you hoping I'd somehow figure something out and force you to do the right thing?"

Scovill rolled his eyes. "Mr. Pilate, you arrogant shit. Cut the psychological bull. I kept you around because I couldn't trust anyone else in this inbred town. You're objective and maybe even intelligent, in spite of your smart-ass tendencies. I just figured you might be someone who could help me."

"Got it. Sorry I held out on you toward the end," Pilate said.

"You had to. You had no idea if you could trust me," Scovill rasped.

"Nah. I knew you were okay," Pilate said. "Sheriff, I have to know something."

"Yeah?"

"Did you know about Rick? That Ollie killed him?"

"Swear to God I had no idea. I suspected later, but at the time, I really thought it was a wreck. You gotta believe me on that, Pilate. Rick was a friend."

"They're going to investigate that big time."

"I did a lot of things wrong, but I never killed anybody," he said, "and I couldn't find any proof that Rick had been murdered. I never profited from any of this. I just couldn't bear to let them say things about my dad."

"I know."

The pair was silent for a moment, the beeping of the monitor filling the void.

"Mr. Pilate, I'm not gonna bullshit you though. For a minute or two...I could've...I could've been on the wrong side of this thing," Scovill said softly, turning his head away from Pilate.

"But you didn't go that way. You did the right thing, in spite of your loyalty to your dad."

"Yeah," he said. He cleared his throat noisily. "My wonderful dad. You know, he did a lot of miserable shit in his life, but he was very good to Mom and me. He was a good dad, just not a good sheriff."

Pilate looked at his hands, noticing he still had some blood caked in his fingernails.

"Well, you better get back to bed before one of those nurses catches you here."

"Sheriff, I'll speak on your behalf to the judge, the papers, everybody," Pilate said.

"Thanks, Mr. Pilate. Maybe they'll go easy on me if an expert burglar and conspiracy-bustin' speech teacher is willing to stand up for me."

Pilate laughed. "You never know." He only managed to walk halfway to the door before Scovill's tired voice called once more.

"John?"

Pilate turned and looked at Scovill.

A single tear tracked from Scovill's squinty eye. "You're a good man—a lousy shot with a Glock, but a good man." He extended a hand a few inches above the sheets, an I.V. tube hanging limply from his wrist.

"Want to know something, Sheriff?" Pilate said.

"What's that?"

"You are too." Pilate shook Scovill's hand.

"Take care of Kate and Kara."

Pilate winked at Scovill and nodded.

By the time Pilate got back to his room with the sugar, the coffee was cold.

The next morning, Pilate got the final onceover from Doc Hutton. "You're coming along pretty well, John," the doctor said, writing on his chart.

"Thanks. I feel better, I think."

Hutton looked up from his chart. "Anything you want to talk about?"

Pilate looked at him quizzically.

"Your mother told me on the phone. They're your closest kin, and the college had their number in your employment records. When we brought you in, we called your folks to get your blood type, medications, etcetera."

"I see," Pilate said.

"Your mother said you've been taking antidepressants, but we know you haven't. How long have you been off your meds?"

"Too long, I think."

Hutton scratched out a prescription. "I have some samples." He handed Pilate the prescription. "Hang on. I'll get some for you."

Pilate went to the bathroom, urinated, and looked at his reflection in the mirror.

Simon appeared at his shoulder. *"Finally, a wise decision, John,"* Simon said.

"I wish I could say I'll miss you," he said.

"Oh, you will." He folded his arms. *"Not right away, mind you…"* All of Simon's body faded away except for his smile, a dysthymic Cheshire cat. *"…but you will."*

PILATE'S CROSS

CHAPTER TWENTY-TWO

Two days later, Pilate was recuperating at home, Kate serving as his vigilant nursemaid.

She brought him the latest *Cross Courier.* It was chockfull of stories about the killings, the conspiracy, the heroic stranger in town who broke it wide open, and even the connection to the Bernard murders.

According to the paper, Grif had been arrested for conspiracy in the death of an unidentified boy in 1963. Divers found traces of the boy's skeletal remains, partially buried in the mud at the bottom of the Missouri, still chained inside the hulk of the stolen Chevy.

Craig Olafson's accomplice, Steve, was caught speeding out of the county in a stolen car by none other than Trooper Hulsey. Steve was high on meth and gave up without a fight.

Scovill was still in the hospital. The county attorney signaled that he would probably proffer charges soon. Cleared of all wrongdoing, Deputy Lenny was now acting sheriff.

A banner headline read *"LINDSTROM OUT."* He had been removed as Cross College president; an interim president would be named any day. Lindstrom wasn't under arrest, but the county attorney, the FBI, and the state police were questioning him. In a photo below the headline, Lindstrom's wife stoically endured the flash of cameras as the pair left the sheriff's office.

"I guess Kara won't be taking any piano lessons this year," Kate said.

Pilate nodded and noted that Cross College Foundation Director Dick Shefler was also being questioned for what the newspaper referred to as *"suspicious activities not in keeping with his fiduciary responsibilities."*

"And I guess Dick won't be running for governor anytime soon," Pilate said, smirking.

"Grif is selling the mortuary," Kate said, removing Pilate's old shoulder bandage. "He thinks he's going to jail, and he wants me and Kara to have her inheritance," Kate said as she applied Neosporin and fresh gauze to Pilate's shoulder. "There's a big chain that's been trying to buy him out for years."

"What will you do then, moneybags?"

Kate finished rolling the bandage around his arm and shoulder, secured it with tape, and helped Pilate lean back on the couch. She kissed his mouth, her hand gently tracing the bandage on his cheek. She pulled away from Pilate, looking into his eyes. "It all depends on what you want to do," she said.

Pilate blinked twice, surprised to discover that he felt peaceful and calm for the first time in years. *Perhaps it's the Percocet.* "Kate, I have to tell you some things about me first, but before I do, I want you to know that nothing would make me happier than to—"

His sentence was interrupted by the telephone ringing.

"Hold that thought," she said. "Hello?"

Kate listened a moment. "Abbey, he's fine."

Kate stayed with Pilate for several days, helping get him up and down from the couch to the bathroom or his bed.

When Kate was at work, Abbey Prince helped out, and she insisted on bringing starchy casseroles every other day.

The first time Kate left the pair alone, Abbey spent a few minutes chatting, then kissed Pilate's cheek and thanked him for "being so brave and inspirational." She smelled of lilacs.

Kate met Pilate's parents when they came up to see him for a couple of days; as his mother had put it, they wanted to "make sure our Johnny is all right." Pilate had to practically beg them not to come any sooner, as they were apoplectic from the hospital call the night of the shooting. Kate liked them, though, and Pilate was pretty sure they approved of her as well. He couldn't imagine anyone not liking Kate.

Riley Pierson and other students checked on him every few days. Riley said he was writing a speech about his new hero, Mr. Pilate.

Pilate asked him what he thought of Abbey Prince.

"She's wicked hot."

On the sixth day, Pilate managed to get up and down on his own. Weary of being the recovering gunshot victim, he decided to be constructive and wash the dishes.

Kate came in from work, kissed his cheek, and leaned against the cabinet next to him. "So," she said, "are you planning on sticking around for a while?"

"Sure. Where else would I go? Interim President Trevathan says my job is safe, all the bad guys are dead and buried or in jail, and there's a really sexy adjunct instructor I want to get to know better."

"I hear she has a spectacular ass," Kate said.

"Well, yeah. That too," Pilate said. "I think I love her."

"Is that you talking or these?" Kate said, holding one of the dozen or so bottles of antidepressant samples Dr. Hutton had given him.

"It's me," he said, "with just a little help from my friends."

"But you're taking these pills," she said. "I mean, I know you need them, but maybe they're clouding your judgment a little, especially since you just started taking them again."

Pilate shrugged, filling the kitchen sink with dirty dishes. "Doesn't matter. I have strict orders to take them."

"From the doc?"

"Yeah…and someone else."

"Who? Your Mom?"

"No. Let's just say that Simon says."

She looked confused.

Pilate turned on the warm and cold water.

Kate smiled and pointed at the answering machine, its red light blinking. "Samantha keeps calling you," Kate said. "She's left a dozen messages on the machine since the news broke."

"I know. I'm not calling her," Pilate said, looking at the water flowing from the tap. "She'll figure it out. It's over. I've moved on."

"Are you sure?"

He smiled, winked, and put his hands under the warm water of the tap. "Rest assured, John Pilate has washed his hands of the whole thing."

EPILOGUE

Their bulky bodies crammed into ornate caskets, Ollie and Craig Olafson were buried in Monticello Cemetery, not far from the Nathaniel family tomb they had desecrated. Family members shed tears as gaudy wreaths leaned crookedly on their stands in the snow.

In Vetsville, the body of Derek Krall was unceremoniously shoved into a new crematory, the only one functioning in the area since Nathaniel's had been put up for sale. Jets of flame consumed the flimsy cardboard coffin and his body, releasing his soul.

Finding no takers for disposition of Krall's ashes, the funeral director slid the warm cardboard box of cremains onto the shelf in a storage room and pulled the chain on the naked light bulb.

THE END

PILATE'S CROSS

J. ALEXANDER GREENWOOD

John Pilate returns in

PILATE'S KEY

CPSIA information can be obtained
at www.ICGtesting.com
Printed in the USA
BVHW032003301120
594533BV00008B/294